SHARING

BOOK THREE OF THE SONG OF THE SEA

SHARING

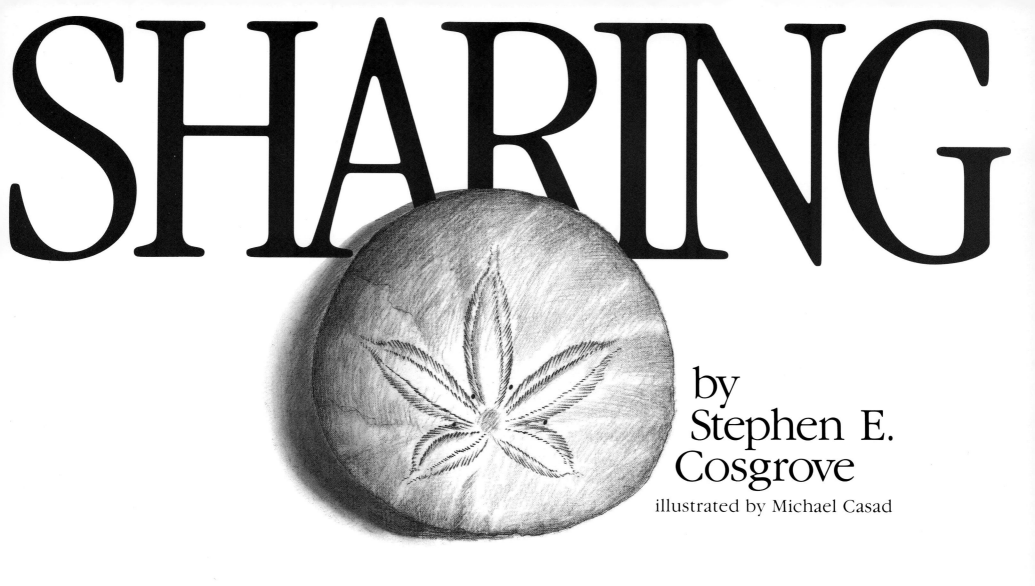

by
Stephen E.
Cosgrove

illustrated by Michael Casad

Graphic Arts Center Publishing Company

Portland, Oregon

BOOK THREE OF THE SONG OF THE SEA

International Standard Book Number 1-55868-066-7
Library of Congress Number 91-71221
Text © MCMXCI by Stephen E. Cosgrove
Illustrations © MCMXCI by Michael Casad
All rights reserved.
No part of this book can be reproduced by an means
without written permission of the publisher.
Published by Graphic Arts Center Publishing Company
P.O. Box 10306 • Portland, Oregon 97210 • 503/226-2402
Editor-in-Chief • Douglas A. Pfeiffer
Managing Editor • Jean Andrews
Designer • Becky Gyes
Typographer • Paul O. Giesey/Adcrafters
Printer • South China Printing Co.
Printed and bound in Hong Kong

*There has come into my life an individual who taught
and continues to teach me to share with ALL THAT IS RIGHT IN THE WORLD.
There is Harmony within her, for her life
is filled with Laughter Ring, and truly she is . . . Sharing.
This book, as well as my life, is dedicated to Nancy Louise Smith.*
Stephen

CONTENTS

*"Like a wave crashing on the coral sands . . .
so shall ye become part and measure of the Song of the Sea."*
as sung to the pod by
Philosophy
in the tide 5345

PASTORAL

I have been to the conclave—a gathering of the greatest minds on earth—and none of those minds were of man. None of those who were present has ever walked the shores of the waters of life, nor has any of them ever envied those who do.

I have been with Harmony. I have argued my case before a tribunal that invokes no harm, but, by its inaction, can enact the greatest punishment of all . . . extinction. I have been with the poets, and now I must teach man to sing again.

The night is not bright, but well lit nonetheless, in this early northern fall. Cotton-gauze clouds filter the half-moon light as I walk my silent walk. Mercury waves slip and slide like long, twisty snakes, hissing up and down the pebbled shore. The air, cool and crisp, bites at my cheeks and explodes into silver vapor streamers as I exhale my breath long-held. This is Alaska September, fall in a place of early hard winter. I look back to where the gravelly shore refuses to mark my passing with lingering bootprints. It is as if I were placed where I am coming from—nowhere—having nowhere to go.

I am now of the Song of the Sea, for I have heard it sung. I am the one in billions of humankind who must try to teach the others to sing. Should I fail to do so, mankind will earn the punishment it has so freely passed on to others . . . extinction. Like my bootprints, we will leave no trace on the jagged edge of the dryside near the waters of life.

I am the wrong with ALL THAT IS RIGHT IN THE WORLD. I am sandwalker, called Sharing by the dolphins who taught me to listen. Sharing—a name given to me late in life by those creatures I have come to love. Sharing—an odd name for one who really hasn't shared at all. Only now have I begun to learn that life is a precious gift. It requires, even demands, that lives be spent giving back the gift to ALL THAT IS RIGHT IN THE WORLD.

Shamed am I—knowing now what I know—penitent for the wrongs that my fellow creatures and I have committed against the sea. I am sandwalker . . . the creatures given so much in the beginning. I am sandwalker . . . the takers of all that can be taken. From birth, we are obsessed with our own mortality; we claw at life, demanding that it give up the secret to eternal youth.

We think ourselves the grandest of creatures. Now it seems that we were grand only in our conceit of dominion of all that we felt we commanded. I am one with these creatures that stagger on the shore, seeking immortality. But I now am also one with the Song of the Sea.

The Song of the Sea, now listened to and understood, boils in my blood. Life takes on new passions with which I am now filled. I am wracked with envy of those who live in the sea, for I do not, and cannot, live there though I crave to do so. I am sandwalker, and to be sandwalker is to envy and covet all that you are not.

The Song of the Sea has few requirements, but one dictate is that the singer, the recorder of the history of a pod, must always identify his or her position in the song. I have been called to record the song for my pod, for the sandwalker . . . for mankind. Therefore, as the song requires, as the song dictates . . . I begin at my beginning.

The most glorious expression of life in the Song of the Sea is birth. Yet we, of all the creatures that live upon the earth, cannot remember the moment of our own beginning. We try. We want to remember, but all bits of this wondrous event seem to be scrubbed clean from our slate of memory, replaced by the initial feeble scratchings of our profound desire to survive.

I am called Sharon . . . born in the turbulent tides that flow without water on the dryside.

My story begins . . . I was born, but I don't remember.

My first memories of life are of muted rainbows that wrapped the world in sunset and dawn and changed blink by blink. I vaguely remember lying in my crib, gazing through the bars to watch a riot of colors and subtle movements that fought for my strictest attention. I remember waking to the gentle touch of a breeze through an open window and the subtle warmth of a sunlight ribbon lancing bright and bold. I remember the joy and reflections of laughter in my parents' eyes at my first hesitant steps. I remember their pain as they looked on my world of silent still. For I was born deaf.

What an odd word . . . deaf. A brief word, a bleak word created by those who can hear. A word

signifying nothing. I do not envy sound. I do not cry or lament my lack. For having never experienced sound, how do I covet it? I have been pitied by nearly all I have met for my seeming lack of ability. But nature compensates, and my compensation was to feel emotion—to truly know the meaning of empathy. I have gone through life sensing without hearing all the music and the riot of sounds around me. I prefer my silence to the seemingly cheap carnival of sounds that hearing folk jostle to experience.

I was taken to the best doctors in the world. Each, upon examining me, found the same thing. Where most are born with a complete inner ear, I, instead, possessed an odd growth of bone that blocked all sound. I could feel vibration, but there was nothing to amplify the tonal qualities. They remained simple vibrations—no sound. My parents tried and tried but finally resigned themselves to that which I had never questioned, for it was simply a part of me . . . I was deaf.

At an early age, my parents compensated for my lack by teaching me to *sign*—to speak the magic language of hand and body. I learned also how to read books much earlier than a so-called *normal* child and was mesmerized by the magic of words. Still and all, signing is more expressive, and to that end—although I can read lips and feel the vibrations of sound—I would much rather paint my words on the wind than make the guttural utterances of *normal* folk.

When I was four and very full of my own directions, my parents took me to the ocean. Oh, what a delight! Breezes, edged lightly with sharp, scented salts, abraded my face and made me feel alive. Boiling waters rolled powerfully to the shore in great arms, then fists, then fingers outstretched, reaching for all and anything that came near. I wanted to go. I was compelled to walk as deep into the water as I could and then to swim farther still. The sea made me laugh. The sea made me cry.

It is as if I were placed where I am coming from —
nowhere — having nowhere to go.

At first sight, I was obsessed with a longing to be a part of this vastness.

And so, in my childlike simplicity of thought, action and deed became one, and I simply sank into the sea. The water boiled before my eyes, and I could not truly see anything but bits of swirling sand. There was a power in the sea that I could not hear, but rather felt. I was shocked, for this was the first time that I truly *felt* sound. I felt the sea roaring, and that word took on new meaning. I felt the sea pound at the land, as in a battle fought from great distances. My journey was shortened by my father as he dashed into the water to save his daughter from drowning in her own delight.

He yanked me, most unceremoniously, from the salty water. Like some prize dangling from his arms, he took me from my sea. As we splashed back to the beach, he clutched me to his hairy chest. I could feel his heart beating, an engine still fueled with the adrenaline of fear. I could not explain to either of my parents what I felt that day. The beauty and the power of the sea were mine to possess—and mine alone. Greedily, I looked upon my domain—my sea. For the

first time, I felt clean . . . absolutely clean and washed over. I didn't want to leave, and I remember that I threw a fit as we drove away from the immediate shore. They laughed at first, then became distressed by my new-found obsession.

Pouting, my lower lip extended in defiance, I sullenly rode with them to our other holiday adventures, paled now by comparison to the sea. Still later in the day, there came a surprise that almost superseded the grandeur of the sea. My parents took me to a place where the ocean fishes were kept in great windowed tanks filled with volumes of water. Here, I could easily view the majesty of life beneath the sea. As a child, I could almost sense what it was like to live beneath the waters. My mother, father, and I went hand in hand from window to window, gazing at this sparkling world. Octopus, parrot fish, cod, and shark all swam together in a mighty synergism. One by one or in milling swarms, they swam by *my* window, occasionally stopping to look at me through the glass, into my world as I looked into theirs. Oh, the delight, the joy!

The tantrum I threw at being torn from the sea was nothing to the one I threw when my parents tried to take me from my window back to our world. My world being soundless, I felt, nonetheless, the discomfort of the other aquarium visitors as I vented my frustration at leaving my new-found friends, the fishes. Out of embarrassment, my mother finally relented and allowed me to stand alone for a few more moments at what was now clearly my window. My parents moved away, all the while keeping a cautious eye on their now wayward daughter who had become a bit obsessed. Sometimes being deaf lent an aura of mystery to an otherwise typical child and softened some punishments to pity.

I stood there, looking through the glazed glass into a world as silent as mine. The minions continued to swim in parade—revue as it were—and I would have watched forever, had it not been for a magical marshmallow monster. Peering into the gloom, seeking to see farther into its depths, my reverie was shattered by a large creature seemingly made of white bubble gum, black eyes scrunched in merriment. This monster seemed to rise from the bottom of the tank as I was looking up. One moment, it wasn't there, and the next, it was. I screeched my immediate fear but continued to watch in rapt fascination. When I could take no more, I ducked down below the glass and, after catching my breath, gripped the moist metal frame and peeked back into the tank. The monster was gone. I stood, shaken by the surprise of it all, when up popped the monster again. Down I ducked; and, as I ducked, I noticed that the monster did the same.

It is miraculous how quickly a child can convert from fear to fascination, and I was no exception. I popped up—the monster popped up. I dropped down—the monster disappeared. I thought to catch this creature in the act. I slowly peeped one eye above the frame to watch its monstrous head rise into view. As slowly as I rose, so rose the monster until I was looking into the heart of his very merry eye. Captured whole by this delight of the deep, I looked into his soul and found so much depth of heart and compassion that I cried for want of never leaving.

In a burst of bubbles, this most unlikely monster backed off so I could see all of him. He was nearly fifteen feet long and pearly white from the tip of his bubbled head to the end of his tail. He cavorted for me there, this priceless crown prince of the teasing sea. I could feel my laughter welling in bursts of giggles as I watched my new-found friend twist and turn, swimming sideways and upside down, all for my delight. Without my notice, my parents had joined me and watched in fascination. Father signed that this delightful creature was whale and, letter by letter, spelled out the word *Beluga*. Beluga whale—a perfect name for my marshmallow monster.

I was captured that day, as only a four-year-old can be, and I pledged myself for all time to the sea. Many, many years later at my college graduation, I stood on the dais and signed the word . . . *Beluga*. Only my parents understood the reference to a very funny whale who, for whatever reason, sought to make a deaf girl laugh.

My childhood, a blur of delights and dilemmas, was the same as that of other children. I worked through special schools for the deaf and persevered my way through college. Painstakingly,

I learned to read lips and, by overarticulating my own speech, to make others understand me. I signed to those who understood that beautiful language; and to those who did not, I appeared the idiot, the dummy, the fool. Through determination alone, I managed to achieve my doctorate in marine biology.

❧

After graduation, I petitioned school after school for a teaching position, but few wanted to risk hiring a deaf professor. In desperation and with a passionate desire to put my love for the sea to some application, I interviewed for the position of staff biologist with a small marina near Los Angeles. My folks tagged along to help translate my signing and to buffer the first shock felt by most people when they interview a deaf person.

Other than my childhood memories of marine parks, I was somewhat ambivalent about the entertainment value of the creatures of the sea. My childhood memory of the Beluga and the other delightful creatures at the aquarium was overshadowed by a sense of melancholy as I followed a teenage guide to the management offices of the marina. Sad-eyed dolphins watched dolefully from tiny concrete pens as we clattered our way through this hodge-podge collection from the sea. In the largest pen at the center of it all, surrounded by carnival pennants and bunting, was a glass-paneled tank where a Beluga, not unlike my whale from years gone by, gently floated. As his winking, gleeful eye peeked at me through the viewing window, I knew that no matter which job was available, it was here I would stay.

The heat of this hot summer's day reflected blindly off the artificially blued waters in tank after concrete tank. My parents and I were led into the office of the owner and manager of this ocean carnival, Dr. Melvin Lambert. His office was cool and dim in contrast with the grounds and smelled of stale cigars, sweat, and cloying cologne. In the middle of the room was a cluttered desk with a goose-neck lamp that spilled light over a paper mountain of receipts, other applications, and candy wrappers. Behind the desk sat Dr. Lambert himself in an overstuffed chair. His tousled hair framed a walrus-looking face, complete with a bushy moustache that wrapped about his mouth. He gave the impression of being eccentric but harmless—harmless, that is, until he opened his mouth.

My father explained to Lambert that although I was deaf I could read lips as well as most people could hear, as long as the person speaking enunciated clearly. Lambert instantly began to overenunciate every word, patronizing me from the start. I had promised myself that I would maintain a sense of professionalism throughout the proceedings, but Lambert's first question nearly shook my resolve, "Well, little girl, why do you want to work at a marina?"

I signed and my father interpreted my slightly idealistic and overly prepared answer, "I want to work at a marina because I love all creatures of the sea. Through research, I feel I can add something, at least my understanding, to the world around me."

The little walrus rolled his beady eyes and threw his chubby arms up, "Oh, Lord!" he laughed, "as I live and breathe . . . another world-saving environmentalist!"

I took a deep breath to control my temper. Calmed, I asked in sign if I could write my answers to his questions rather than signing them through my father. Lambert reluctantly agreed, and a performance slate used to train dolphins was acquired. My father went outside to wait with my mother, and I was left alone with this barracuda. For the rest of the interview, I scribbled in response to his interrogation. I am sure it was only by accident that my nails raked across the board as I answered some of his more asinine questions.

"What are you all about?" I often thought
as I sat there, watching the water lap softly
on the backs of these gentle creatures.

At the conclusion of the nearly two-hour interview, Dr. Lambert leaned back in his chair and smiled his little oil-slick smile. "You know, Shar-oon," he overenunciated, "I really don't like environmentalists. For the most part, they are nothing more than pests that stand in the way of progress. Worse yet, they want to be paid for being pests. If I hire you, I will have you bemoaning the plight of these stupid creatures, these sea-borne beasts of burden. If I don't hire you, then I am a heartless old grouch who won't hire the handicapped."

The chalk fairly danced across the slate as I angrily and boldly wrote, "I AM NOT HANDI-CAPPED!" and my fingernails once again screeched along the slate.

"Hold on! Hold on!" he muttered, probably as much to confuse my lip-reading as to stop my fingernails from further inadvertent abrasion. "There are several things in your favor. Because you are handicapped—pardon me, because you are not handicapped but still are deaf—we'll qualify for some additional government grants. Furthermore, your being on staff would add a bright, new pity angle to our public relations. Hmm, I like that . . . 'THE ONLY MARINA THAT CATERS TO THE DEAF AND OTHER HANDICAPPED.'"

He paused as he noticed my angry expression. "Don't look so shocked! This is the real world, kid; and deaf, dumb, or both, people are going to use you. The reality of life is making money, and that's what *this* is all about," he said, waving his pudgy little hands in a grand sweeping gesture about the room. "It would be a lot simpler just to keep the little fishies, for they don't need much upkeep, and they kind of eat themselves . . . but the paying public wants a circus: they want a show. So, I give them whales and dolphins and sometimes a pretty deaf girl to feel sorry for. They get what they want, and I get what I want. They get to be close to that fat, floating marshmallow called a Beluga, and I

get bigger gate receipts. Well, what do you say, Shar-oon?" he overenunciated. "Do we have a deal?" He extended his greasy right hand with its plump, sausage fingers.

I didn't know what to do. On the one hand, I wanted to grind him up as shark bait, and, on the other, I had a grudging respect for his blunt honesty. I took the job, but I didn't take Lambert's hand. With facades firmly back in place, we went out into the waiting room to tell my parents the news.

My title was staff marine biologist, but my job was simply to care for the whale and dolphins. Mine was a basic task—to make sure that they were ready for the hourly shows, period . . . nothing else. Any research or study I wanted to do had to be done on my own time, which suited me fine.

My parents helped me find a small, furnished house to rent only a couple of blocks from the marina, and, after moving my clothes and personal things, they left me alone in my new surroundings. Through college and graduate schools, I had still felt like a child, but now, for the first time, I was truly on my own.

So began my daily routine as a professional. For the most part, I steered clear of Lambert for both our sakes and concentrated on the care of the fish, dolphins, and the whale. Helping me was a Native American by the name of Peter Twofin. Peter was a Haida Indian from Alaska who, with his natural abilities, intuition, and rugged strength, was a great help. He bothered me, though, because often I would find him staring at me and he wouldn't look away. He'd grin. I'd scowl. He'd grin again, infec-tiously. And every time, I would smile back, feeling like an idiot, and then I would turn away, cheeks flaming. He was a great help but a bit odd.

Nighttime at the marina was a gentle time when the whale and dolphins quietly swam about their pools and cast longing glances as I sat watching. "What are you all about?" I often thought as I sat there, watching the water lap softly on the backs of these gentle creatures. "Do you think? Do you worry? Do you laugh? Can you read my mind?"

I privately named the Beluga "Pillsbury," and in my nighttime rounds he was my clown prince. Pillsbury was an absolute delight, even if a bit rambunctious. He seemed to know when everyone had left and we were all alone. Then his games would begin, and he would race about the pool in gleeful abandon. But he was old, and, other than simple non-performance appearances at the Marina Revues, he did nothing more than swim idly in his tank and wait for me. It was odd, but there was always a perception of a greater intelligence and soul within the eyes of this Beluga. Since I had been a child, whales' eyes had always danced with a seeming desire to communicate. Now that I was working at the marina, that reaching out—that staring into the soul through the eye—was a daily occurrence.

During my second month at the marina, I began to take note of the training techniques of the infamous Dr. Lambert. If a particular dolphin did not perform to the good doctor's expectations or didn't finish a routine correctly, the animal's food ration was cut in half, Lambert's theory being that a hungry dolphin was a cooperative dolphin. Late at night, I would slip into the tank with fish for the delinquent dolphin, though not enough that Lambert could know anything was amiss.

The punishments inflicted on the dolphins were nothing to the "techniques" used on poor Pillsbury. The doctor was obsessed with the Beluga's failure to do more than swim 'round the performance tank and occasionally breach on command. Lambert had been to the famous marinas like Sea World. There he had seen all that he wished his marina

could become. He would return from a conference in San Diego filled with envy for the others' capabilities and gate receipts.

"What we need," he railed, "is an Orca—a killer whale—a crowd pleaser. Then we could pull in the dough. Big bucks! But can I buy an Orca? No! I have only one big tank, and I can't afford to build any others. That one big tank is filled with a floating fish disposal that can't even burp on command." With hate in his eyes, he would glare over the glass fence. Poor Pillsbury, sensing the mood of his captor, would always swim to the other side of the tank.

Shortly after one of these tirades, I began to notice odd, round welts on Pillsbury's skin. At first, they were only on his dorsal fin, but, as weeks went by, they began to appear on his great snout and around his eyes. He also began to act listless even at nighttime, which used to be filled with great excitement. He would float quietly on the surface of the water, staring glassy-eyed at nothing in particular. I wrote note after note to the other staff members, asking if they knew the cause of the round welts or the lethargy, but Peter and the others seemed as mystified as I.

Even Lambert appeared almost sympathetic about the mysterious lesions. "Tsk," he would mutter as he shook his head, "poor old whale must be butting his head against the tank at night after everybody is gone. Damn! I sure hope he's not getting that beaching virus."

The beaching virus, or whatever it was, caused entire pods of whales to beach themselves—to rush full-speed from the sea to the shore, there to lie until they died. I, too, prayed fervently that it was not this mysterious malady—for the result was always the same . . . death.

Day in and day out, Peter and I checked the inside of the tank for any odd protuberance that could be causing the wounds, but we could find nothing. Nightly, I would scour book after book, but no research could solve the mystery. I would fall asleep at night and wake in the morning worrying about Pillsbury. No matter what I tried, from food supplements to shots of megavitamins, nothing seemed to work. Pillsbury was getting worse and worse. It came to the point where he refused to eat and seemed to give up on life itself. Peter and I began to force-feed him—fish at first, then mixtures of ground protein.

Nearly six weeks after the mystery began, it abruptly ended. I arrived at the marina early, and somehow even to my deaf ears, it seemed muffled, wrapped in a cotton blanket. All the tanks, which normally sloshed and splashed about with the movements of the great creatures inside, were still. I looked first in the dolphin tank. The five creatures, who normally darted about in great anticipation of the morning feedings, lay quiet upon the water. I could feel the quiet—this pervasive stillness.

"Oh, my God!" I thought. "Pillsbury."

I raced down the concrete aisles and up the ramp that wound around the Beluga's tank. The fact that Pillsbury was also motionless in the water didn't frighten me as much as the slackness of his skin and the odd way he was floating. Without hesitation, I leaped fully clothed into the tank. He didn't move. I swam to his side, stroking his long flank in the desperate hope that my worst fears wouldn't be realized. I reached his head, and, for a moment, there was a flutter of life. His great eye opened, scrunched together in that merry wink of his, then grew wide, and with a great exhaust of air from his blowhole—he died.

Never in my life have I felt such grief, such anguish. My bones seemed to vibrate, and my body began to ache. I tried in vain to keep his head above water, but his dead bulk was finally too much. He slowly sank to the bottom. I dove repeatedly, trying to pull him up, but it was all to no avail. How long I stayed in the tank I don't know. Vaguely, I remember Peter pulling me from the water and holding me in consolation. Even Dr. Lambert seemed to be mellowed by the event. Grief-stricken as I was, I allowed him to wrap a spongy arm around me in sympathy. I finally took a deep breath and, with a shudder, accepted the reality of my beloved creature's mortality. After all, Pillsbury had been in captivity for more than fifteen years, and it was only by sheer luck that he had lived as long as he had.

As I composed myself, Lambert began organizing efforts to remove Pillsbury from the tank. A lift was procured from the boat works next door and moved into position. A sling was then guided into the water and, carefully, as if to honor the memory of this whale's past delights, it was slipped beneath the great bulk. He was finally free of his tiny sea, his prison. As they lifted him, I noted new round welts in great profusion all over one side of his head.

The odd thing was that there didn't seem to be a pattern. Part of one welt overlapped his eye, and the lid itself appeared to be burned.

Grabbing my slate, I rushed to Dr. Lambert, who was standing to the side, watching the goings-on. Quickly, I scribbled, "I want to perform an autopsy."

"No," he said, overenunciating his words in his usual way, thinking it helped me read his lips. "That won't be necessary, Shar-oon. You've been through a lot, and I know how much the whale meant to you. Let's just say he died quietly of old age."

I began to write furiously, "But I want to find out what caused his death. What caused the great welts?"

His fat cheeks reddened as he blustered, "Read my lips, little girl! I said, 'No!'"

"Now," he shouted to the crew, "get that carcass out of here."

I stumbled from the tanks and into the office to compose myself. I found some tissue, dried my eyes, and took a deep breath of reality. I was just leaving the office, when I saw an odd, narrow tube sitting on Lambert's desk. It was about two and a half feet long and nearly an inch in diameter.

I carefully picked it up to examine it further. One end had a handlebarlike grip, and the other end was smooth. I idly touched it to my arm, and the resulting shock knocked me to the floor. I lay there dazed and then looked at my arm. A perfectly formed, round welt swelled from the burning of delicate flesh and nerves.

Now I knew the cause of the mysterious disease that had plagued the gentle Beluga . . . greed!

I vowed to bring full revenge to bear on the person responsible for the horrible death of Pillsbury. And obviously, that person was Lambert himself.

I moved quickly, taking whatever measures I felt necessary at the time. Then I waited, for there was nothing more I could do. I would arrive at the marina early in the morning, and I could feel the hollow echoes of my footsteps against Pillsbury's tank. Everything seemed dank, as the fog-shrouded late days of summer reflected the mourning I felt. But revenge would come in its own sweet time. I waited patiently for a fat fish to take the baited hook.

Nearly two weeks later, as I was working in the utility closet that had been converted to lab, office, and operating room, Lambert appeared. Leaning against the door-jamb, he watched me awhile in that affected, bemused style of his. In turn, I stared at him blankly. When

I refused to comment on his presence, he stiffly mouthed, "The staff says that you continue to question the death of the Beluga. They say you took a lot of pictures of the carcass and, even against my wishes, took biopsy samples of the round welts. In addition, there seems to be a special training tool missing from my office. Well, little girl, I want the pictures, the biopsy samples, and the training tool—now. When I have those in hand, I just might not call the police and have you arrested for petty larceny. Instead, you are to pack up and get off the grounds of this marina before I have you thrown off!"

"Doctor," I smiled, attempting to soothe the anxieties I felt, "I will not turn over the pictures of Pillsbury to you, nor will I give you the biopsies. For you see, Dr. Lambert, all tests are completed, and the results, along with the pictures of the injuries themselves, are stored in a safe place. As for the 'training device,' tests have already proven that it was the cause of the mysterious welts and the ultimate death. Now that the tests are finished, you can have it back." I reached into my desk drawer and removed the cattle prod. It must have been accidentally turned on, for as I removed it from the desk and slapped it into Lambert's fleshy hand, it snapped with renewed vigor from the freshly charged batteries. Lambert's eyes opened wide, perhaps in shock of the discovery of the truth: maybe the cattle prod really does hurt.

Lambert stood there, his mouth open, a bit of spittle foamed on his lower lip. "What are you going to do?" He paused, and then blustered, "It was an accident. That's it! An accident. I haven't done anything illegal."

"That, my dear doctor, is a moral argument I don't wish to be involved in. The point is that if the press found out about this, you would get all the free publicity you could ever want to have. If you wish, I will turn the materials over right now."

Lambert began to sweat profusely. "But the report of an accident could bankrupt me!" he wailed. After a long, shuddering breath, he asked, "What do you want me to do?"

"You, Dr. Lambert," I continued, freezing him in his tracks, "are going to do a lot. I know you had the Beluga insured for more than a million dollars. With that money, you are going to build a new surgical room and a laboratory. You are going to improve the holding pens, and, Dr. Lambert, if I ever discover that you are using some sort of *training device* again, the photographs and the test results will go to the press immediately. Do we understand one another?"

He smiled a greasy little smile, licked the palm of his hand that still burned from the cattle prod, nodded, and silently walked away. Three days later, work began on the new surgery and holding pens.

I didn't like having to revert to coercion, lowering myself to Lambert's rock-bottom level. I anguished for some time over our conversation and my ultimate decision. But work continued on the new buildings and holding tank. I have always felt that we are today what we were yesterday, and yesterday I cast a die that maybe was no better than the one Lambert had thrown. At least, from my actions, some good would come for the hapless creatures that fell into the marina's dangerous tanks. I talked at some length with Peter about sending the test results to the press. But in the end, we did nothing more.

Lambert and I avoided one another as much as possible. He knew I was coercing him into improving the lot of these unfortunate creatures, but, for the moment, he bided his time. Several weeks later, greatly agitated, Lambert rushed to me and spun me around as I stood near the shark exhibit.

He began to puff his lips in his odd, exaggerated way, assuming somehow that this contorted speech would help me read his lips.

"Shar-oon, the greatest of great news for sure!" he mouthed. "We've got an Orca!"

There were times throughout my life, for whatever reason, that I pretended to misunderstand what people had said. I like to think I did this to give myself more time to answer complex questions. However, on the devilish side, carefully done, I could get Lambert to repeat himself as many as five or six times as he patiently tried to *talk* to me, the dummy. I shook my head, incredulous, and said, "You're excited because you've got an orchid? I didn't even know you liked flowers."

"Orca, not orchid, you idiot," he sprayed again, "a killer whale who will bring us *mucho dinero*—big bucks. The greatest draw any marina could ask for. The ghost of that old, fat Beluga can leave now—we got ourselves an Orca." With that, he waddled away to pass on the news to the rest of the staff.

Though nothing could take the place of my Pillsbury, I, too, was caught up in the excitement of the new captive. The old tank was destroyed, and, with it, the last vestige of the Beluga's domain. There truly began a fading of memory as new modern tanks and interconnected pools were quickly constructed. Whenever Lambert tried to cut short on quality that would put any of the creatures at risk, I simply stared at him intently, and he was reminded of our "little deal"—a deal, I might add, that wore heavily on my conscience.

His guilt, or rather his fear of complicity, always caused him to capitulate.

The Orca Lambert acquired was purchased from another marina that found itself with too many captives and not enough cash. Lambert had been able to buy this older, trained Orca at far below its market value, if indeed a market value could be placed on such a magnificent creature. Although the whale was coming from another marina, I still feared for his adjustment to unfamiliar surroundings. Construction was geared up to a fever pitch, and crews worked night and day to prepare the new facilities.

Older, smaller tanks were torn down and replaced with bigger, deeper tanks. Lambert even rebuilt the grandstands to seat the larger audiences he anticipated. When the new tanks were finished, they were quickly filled with fresh seawater and sterilized to minimize any chance of infection.

By this time, my personal staff had increased twofold. I was able to add two additional part-time college students, which, counting Peter and myself, brought my staff to four. We all rushed about, moving equipment into the new laboratory, much to the chagrin of workmen who were still trying to finish the structure itself. Peter continued his odd smiling routine, and often I would look up and catch him staring at me with that silly grin on his face. I'd frown, shake my head, and turn away before the twinkle in his eye became too infectious.

Peter Twofin aside, all went well. It was my plan to give the Orca at least sixty days to acclimate himself to his new surroundings before submitting him to the strain of training for performances. Lambert and I locked horns repeatedly about this issue, and only after a bit of compromise on my part did he relent to give me thirty days to settle my new charge.

The whale arrived by flat-bed truck. He was wrapped in water-saturated material to keep his skin moist and prevent dehydration. Even so, on his arrival, his dorsal, the great sail-fin, was drooping nearly to the bed of the truck. With the aid of a rented crane, he was lifted carefully up and lowered into a small holding pen where my staff and I waited.

The water level rose as his great bulk was lowered into the tank. He was a beautiful specimen. Because of the afternoon heat and the debilitating journey, Peter ran hoses into the tank and poured cooling waters over the Orca's back. With hands on rubbery skin, we massaged, more, it seemed, to console ourselves than for any aid we could give this behemoth. Slowly, we felt his body begin to undulate as he twisted and began to move. He swam around the narrow confines of the holding pen, and I was amazed at his ability to turn in tight circles.

After hours of constant observation, I felt that he could safely be shifted to the larger tank, the concrete pen that was to be his home for a long time to come. The gates were opened, and, alone, I maneuvered him into the larger pen.

Purposely, I had placed two of our five dolphins in the pen for companionship and to act as a buffer to the shock of transfer. Oddly, I could feel the sound when the dolphins chittered excitedly as we moved into the tank. The Orca seemed to respond in kind with a low vibration that gave me goose bumps on my arms and legs.

I ducked my head beneath the water, and, to my surprise, I felt the vibrations again, only stronger. It wasn't just a vibrating sensation on my skin, but a rhythmic, tonal buzzing in my head. In all my life, I had never heard a sound; I had only felt vibration. This was different. This seemed intelligent. This was an attempt at communication.

The old Orca's eye scrunched as if to smile, and, with one more buzz, he swam to his new companions. I popped from the water and signed to Peter, "Did you hear that?"

He looked at me oddly. "No, I didn't hear a thing. Besides," he laughed, "you can't hear anyway."

"I know I can't hear," I signed sheepishly, "but I felt a strong vibration. You're sure you heard nothing?"

At the edge of the pen, I could see Lambert asking somebody what I said. Then he laughed, and, moving his lips slowly, he contorted, "Maybe the whale has gas."

Perplexed, I slipped again beneath the water, staring at my new charge. I waited for the sensation to occur again, but nothing happened. Then, a moment later, came a short, intense vibration. Then all was still. Although I stayed in the water for more than an hour, there were no more vibrations.

What was the feeling—the buzzing in my inner ear? Was the whale trying to communicate?

REFRAIN

Celebration of my discovery was diluted by a sense of disbelief. Everyone since the ancient Greeks has wanted to believe that water-borne mammals can communicate. Claim after claim had proven to be based on an overactive imagination, or even fraud.

So for now, I chalked my experience up to imagination alone.

But the impression I got whenever I looked in the eye of this new whale was one of intelligence and a haunting belief that he was attempting to communicate. I didn't feel it was a matter of him not understanding us, but rather a matter of us not understanding him. Often throughout my college career, I had read about experts who equated the intelligence of dolphins and whales with that of clever dogs and other domestic pets. But there was soul in those eyes, not the mindless innocence of a kitten or puppy. It was rather the bemused merriment of an intelligent being, delighting in all the joys of life.

I spent all my free time in or near the new tank, but never felt the vibrating sensation outside the tank. Only when I was in the water proper, and then only when my head was submerged, did the sensation return. When approached by the great Orca, I would feel in my inner ear a vibration, like a tuning fork long-since struck. Oh, how I wanted to believe that in some small part I was truly hearing for the first time, but the sensation was not sound. It was vibration.

Late one night when the park had closed, I again stood on the observation platform and stared into the translucent, black eyes of the whale. There was that depth, that feeling of soul, of great intelligence, of compassion.

"What are you?" I signed, "some mythical, magical creature—or a grand figment of my imagination? Why can't you speak? Why don't you speak and shock man's world to its very foundations?"

My reverie was broken by an abrupt movement of the whale. He lurched forward, sending a great cascade of water sloshing over the platform. The rush was so great that I lost my footing and fell bone-jarringly onto my butt—my legs extended in front of me over the water. Time all but stopped as I watched the great, sharp-toothed mouth of the Orca open and bite down on my feet. Knowing the strength of those jaws, I realized it would only be a moment before I would be a meal for this "killer whale." When I tried to pull back, the whale clamped down firmly on my feet and yanked me into the water.

Being deaf, I don't know how much noise I made, but my mouth was open wide and I was forcing a lot of air out in a panicked attempt at communication. Whatever, as I hit the water, the whale released my feet, and I sputtered to the surface, gulping air on top of the water I had already swallowed. I spun like a top in the water, looking for my assailant, prepared to defend myself to the end. How could I ward off a multi-ton attacker?

I spit the water from my mouth, and finally my eyes cleared. There, not four feet away, was the Orca, complacently watching me. Certain that he was prepared for another attack, I began to gently back-paddle to the edge of the tank, but as I moved, he moved. Only a few more feet and I would be within arm's reach of the platform and safety. I backed up farther, but this time I felt resistance and was pushed back toward the whale.

My God! The dolphins were working in concert with the whale. Never in all my studies had I ever read that dolphins helped killer whales in their feeding. Great! My first major

discovery as a biologist, and the knowledge would never be consumed by my peers. Rather, my discovery and my body would be digested in a more bizarre manner in the belly of a very intelligent whale.

I turned to the side and started to swim parallel to the dolphin at my back and the whale in my face, but I was blocked again by another of the dolphins. Trapped as I was, the only avenue of escape seemed to be down. I dove quickly and nearly made my escape when I felt the deep, rhythmic vibrations in my inner ear. The buzzing was gentle and soothed my feelings of fear. This didn't seem to be the cry of a blood-hungry whale about to devour his first manwich.

I surfaced, confused but still alive. The whale had quietly submerged, and as my head rose from the water, so did his. It was a standoff. Suddenly, my attention was diverted to the other side of the tank and the welcome sight of Peter's lopsided grin. He crudely signed, "Are you okay?"

I turned and looked at my attackers. None was threatening, but neither were they moving back. I carefully raised my arms from the water and signed, "I was in danger. I am now safe, for the moment. Watch carefully for any signs of threat." I turned back to the whale, whose eyes seemed to twinkle in the artificial lights of the marina park. He slowly dropped his massive head back under the water, and the dolphins did the same. I waited a moment or two, and then they all popped back to the surface. They slowly sank again, and again I waited. Again, they bobbed to the surface in unison. Peter looked at me, questioningly now, with a formidable spear gun cradled in his arm—cocked and ready.

I hand-spoke to him to stay where he was but to put the gun

I realized it would only be a moment
before I would be a meal for this "killer whale."

away. Inwardly, I was very relieved that he was there. If you are about to give your life for science, literally as lunch, there's always a sense of relief that someone will at least know where you have disappeared to. I turned back to the center of the tank.

The process of the bobbing mammals happened three more times, and I swear the whale and dolphins were getting frustrated that I didn't understand what was going on. Once again, in unison, they dropped below the surface, and again I was alone with the ripples. I looked to Peter, who was now nervously watching this odd behavior from the platform, gun at the ready.

Suddenly, I felt a tug at my foot, and before fear or alarm, I was suddenly drawn beneath the water back to my position in the food chain. I was a bit more prepared this time, and at least my mouth was closed. The grip was not uncomfortable, but I definitely was being held under the water. But why? Once again, the rhythmic vibrations began, and I was soothed. Then the pulsations stopped. My leg was released, and I popped to the surface like a cork. With me came my errant new playmates, who watched expectantly. Peter urgently signed from the platform, "What's happening? Why are you dipping up and down in the water?"

I returned in sign, "I don't know what's happening, but for some odd reason, they, the dolphins and the whale, want me under the water." I thought for a moment as I floated in the water—me watching them watching me. There was a device we had been using called a tonal analyzer that recorded all sounds on a paper graph. It was the one tool essential to my research of mammal intelligence that, as a deaf person, I would be lost without. I signed to Peter to turn on the machine and begin recording.

When he was ready, I again dropped beneath the surface of the water. Sure enough, the whale and dolphins did the same. And, as before, the pulsations came, wrapping their soothing arms around me. Again, when the vibrations stopped, I surfaced quickly and signed to Peter for the reading. To my chagrin, he said that other than standard background chirping, there was nothing recorded.

The dolphins merrily bobbed their heads and tossed water in my face. Once again, I slipped beneath the surface, followed by the vibrations. When I rose again to the surface, as before, a perplexed Peter signed that there was no signal. What was this? What was happening? Had I lost my mind?

The dolphins and whale moved closer, but there was nothing in their movement that I perceived as threatening. If anything, there was a sense of bonding. I signed to Peter to throw me a pair of goggles and a snorkel. He was gone but a minute and tossed the gear high in the air. They landed neatly in front of me, throwing a splash of water into my face.

I pulled the mask on and bit down on the mouthpiece. All secured, I submerged just far enough that the snorkel was barely exposed to the surface. The creatures of the sea, satisfied that I was under to stay and not about to pop up again, also submerged. We floated there, suspended between two alien worlds. As before, my inner ear rang with the rhythmic buzzing. It stopped, then started again, and there was a definite pattern to it.

One of the dolphins swam from the others and isolated himself in front of me. I reached out in the water and touched the side of his head. Then, slowly, the rhythm of the buzzing changed. This process was repeated over and over until it suddenly dawned on me that the rhythms were distinct. At the same time, the dolphin was arching his body, turning into himself. Was the vibration I was feeling the dolphin word for dolphin?

Shocked though I was, I carefully signed, "Dolphin."

Strong hands reached down and grabbed me under
my arms and lifted me from the water.
I collapsed, sobbing at the edge of the pool.

The whale and the others all called rhythmically in unison, "Dolphin. Dolphin. Dolphin."

In turn, spinning in the water, I too signed, "Dolphin! Dolphin! Dolphin!"

They speak!

I stayed in the water, learning and teaching the rudimentary basics of language. The dolphin and the whale both spoke, but the oddity was that, of the two, the whale spoke richer, more philosophically. The dolphin spoke of sillier things and refused, at times, to concentrate on all that was going on. It wasn't that their patience was thin, but they disliked subjects that weren't glittering or plump with potential for a good joke.

They all watched as I signed for one thing or another in the tank. Then the rhythmic buzzing would translate, and I would know the equivalent word in their language. Language—how quickly I changed from calling it buzzing and vibration in my inner ear to language. The sea creatures must have listened and spoken to man for hundreds of thousands of years. We just didn't know how to listen.

They taught me the simple words for the water and life itself. They taught the word "dryside"—the side above the waters of life. They taught of the feathered furies, the birds who fly on the winds of the dryside. And, oh yes, they don't call us man. They call us the sandwalker, he who walks on the dryside.

They taught me so much in a short time, but it was only a grain of sand on the greatest beach of all. Whales and dolphins have been on this earth longer than man, and, from what I understand, they have a recorded history that has been passed on by exacting memory. Oh, that man was not a slave to labor-saving devices! In our cleverness, we forget to remember and, instead, rely on inventive devices.

I came from the water reluctantly, for I needed teaching tools and pictorial aids. I excitedly signed to Peter, "Did you record all of that?"

He looked at me, perplexed, his face screwed up. "Record what?" he asked in mouth-speak.

"The conversation." I waved with my hands as I laughed and danced about, "Man's first conversation with—excuse me—the sandwalker's first conversation with his intellectually superior and older cousins, the whale and dolphin."

Peter stared at me intently, concern overriding his normal sarcastic wit. "Did you strike your head when the whale dragged you beneath the water? Sharon, come here and look at the tape."

I walked to the analyzer. I must have looked the fool, sopping wet in my clothes and a snorkel and goggles strapped to my head. I looked at the tape, expecting to see a wide, pulsing graph showing a variety of modulation. Instead, I found only the normal subtle rises and falls. "This can't be right," I signed. Impatiently, I fussed with the machine, but still the analyzer showed that neither the whale nor the dolphins had made any recordable sound at all.

Peter grabbed me by the shoulders and spun me around, "Look, Doc, the tape even shows the minor fluctuations of your motions in the water as you were making all those bizarre signings. I mean, what were you signing? sand . . . walker—sand . . . walker? What did that mean?"

I asked incredulously, "You couldn't record or hear the whale speaking to me?"

He patronizingly began to overenunciate as he spoke, "Sharon, read my lips. There was nothing to record. You were underwater, signing to the whale and the two dolphins. They didn't respond. They floated beneath the water like inflatable pool toys and watched you sign obscure word combinations like dry, side, fury, feathered, waters, and life. I swear to you, they didn't chirp or squeak anything they haven't always done in their delightfully stupid animal way. You must have bumped your head and gotten a minor concussion. You were having a delusion caused by the blow to your head. Come on, let me drive you to the hospital."

I shrugged off his conciliatory hand on my shoulder. "I don't need the hospital. I know what I heard," I declared.

He turned his head from side to side. "Watch what you are saying," he said patiently. "'I know what I heard.' Sharon, you are deaf. Stone-deaf since birth. You wouldn't know the difference between a splash in the water and a shotgun blast."

Tears welled from my eyes in frustration. I knew what I had felt in the water. I knew what I had heard deep within my inner ear. True, it was not sound or what sound should possibly be like, but I heard it! They spoke with me. Shaken to my very core, I meekly allowed Peter to take me to the emergency room of the local hospital. I barely remember the doctor telling me that I had suffered some form of traumatic shock and was hallucinating. He smiled, chuckling joyfully as he walked away from his patient who "spoke with whales."

I was not crazy. I had suffered no trauma other than the powerful shock of new-found knowledge and my amazing discovery. The whale did speak!

Peter took me home and mother-henned me with a cup of hot tea. Again, I acquiesced to his demands, slipped into a robe, and sat quietly in a chair sipping the steaming beverage. Satisfied that I was all right, he left. I watched as he pulled out of the driveway in his pick-up, then I put the teacup in the sink. Still dressed in my robe, I walked the few blocks back to the marina and the whale.

The night security guards were amused at my dress, but because I had often come in the middle of the night to make observations, they didn't bar my entry. I rushed back to the tank, robe flapping about my legs, my still-bare feet stinging as they slapped the walkways in hurried determination.

All my doubts were smoothed away when the whale reared his mighty head above the edge of the tank, and, once again, I looked into his great eye. Anyone who looks into the eye of a whale or a dolphin will see the depth of soul and intelligence that is there. Without thought, I leaped, robe and all, back into the tank. I signed, "Dolphin . . . dolphin," and ducked my head beneath the water.

But all was still. I bobbed from the water, dragging deep mouthfuls of night air into my tortured lungs. I signed, "Whale . . . whale." Once again, I plunged my head beneath the water. I waited and waited, but the whale sat motionless, staring with those great, unblinking eyes. And the water was silent.

Oh, no! It was a dream. Never have I felt so lost. Never have I felt so defeated! I stood shoulder-deep in the water with tears mixing and mingling with the dripping saltwater from my hair. Strong hands reached down and grabbed me under my arms and lifted me from the water. I collapsed, sobbing at the edge of the pool. There was Peter, again kneeling to console me, and also there, the hallucination of all hallucinations, Dr. Lambert.

"Shar-oon," he mouth-spoke and spit, "Don't think this little episode will get you out of work tomorrow. Hee, hee! Though I kind of like the sound of it: DEAF GIRL LISTENS TO WHALE SPEAK. It's got a kind of ring to it. Twofin, take her home and put her back to bed. By the way, Doctor Shar-oon, I really like the robe." With that, he waddled into the night, back to whatever rock he slept under.

"Come on, Sharon," lip-spoke Peter, as he helped me to my feet, "you just need some rest." As I shuffled away from the tanks, I looked back, and there were three heads lifted above the concrete edge.

Like an invalid, I was led out of the marina and into the passenger seat of Peter's truck, which was still damp from my last ride and soon to be wetter still from my sopping robe. "If I had known that I was going to be moving mermaids," he signed, smiling broadly, "I would have gotten plastic seat covers. I feel like I'm driving a goldfish bowl."

I shook my head and let the laughter roll. It was all just a bump on the head, a dream caused by a lonely whale who wanted simply to play with my foot.

❧

I slept that night wrapped in odd dreams of whales and dolphins writing me letters and then denying they had written them. I woke later, confused, not knowing if I had dreamed it all or only part. The sight of my dripping robe and the pool of saltwater on the carpet forced me, in a quantum leap, back to reality. I threw the quilt back over my head and groaned. Lambert had been there. I would never live it down. By now, there would be a reader board out front, entreating people to buy tickets to view the newest exhibit . . . me!

I finally staggered from bed and slurped the now-cold tea Peter had made the night before. I took an ice-cold shower, got dressed, and was just walking out of the house when Peter's pick-up squealed into my driveway. Steeled for the ribbing to come, I was shocked when he signed, "There is an emergency up the coast. Lambert has loaned us to help."

"What happened?" I asked as I piled into the truck.

"Almost a hundred whales are beaching themselves," Peter replied. "Lambert took a helicopter. Thinks he might snag a free whale."

We drove rapidly up the coast. Beachings! A biologist's greatest frustration and a whale lover's greatest fear.

My reverie was broken by our arrival at the beach. There below us, fifty or so whales were simply swimming up onto the beach. I stood there, watching in horrified fascination, awed at the magnitude of the sight of whales throwing themselves to the shore.

Peter and I rushed down to the beach to help in any way we could, and there, waiting for us, was Lambert. "Do what you can," he mouthed. "But remember, you are on my payroll, and if we can save one of these free whales, I want it. Folks will pay to see the whale we saved from the sands of death."

I ignored him as we waded into the surf and, with the others on the beach, began trying to turn this whale-tide back to sea. For the most part, it was futile; they were already dying. A few of the babies were easily turned, but the adults were steadfast

The beginning, like all beginnings, was rudimentary
and primitive. "I am whale, called Dreamer . . . I have
come to the dryside to see what I might see."

in their apparent desire to suicidally throw themselves upon the shore.

In all the confusion, there was an oddness that belied the stark reality. All the members of the pod had thrown themselves on the shore two or three hours before. Not until they were all nearly dead did a great white whale, an albino, come rushing at the shore. Why had he waited? Where was he when the others beached themselves? Was he throwing himself to the shore in grief at the loss of his family and friends?

We pushed and prodded but to no avail as he undulated his way farther and farther from the sea. We had all but given up and resigned ourselves to yet another death when, seemingly from nowhere, there swam two dolphins. Our first reaction was that the dolphins, too, were caught in the contagion, but, to our shock and delight, they began to pull on the tail and fins of the great white, trying to turn him back to sea. Their tugging finally roused the whale from his reverie of death. He turned his great head to look back at these two finned apparitions.

Suddenly, the whale lurched, broadsiding me with his side fin and pulling me under the water. I was rolling to my side to fight my way back to the surface when suddenly I heard once again the rhythmic pulsations . . . the buzzing deep in my inner ear. It wasn't just one single pulse but two, then three separate and distinct rhythms and pulsations, like differences between signatures. I would have forced myself to stay under longer, but the fin that had pulled me into the water now pushed me out. This whale, for whatever reason, had experienced a change of heart and turned back to sea.

I sputtered and cleared my eyes. It was marvelous! Two tiny dolphins had bitten and pulled a great whale from certain death on the shore. As the whale turned, I looked into his eye, and there was not kindness but an anger and rage terribly frightening to behold. There was intelligence. There was soul. And there was pain . . . pain of a sort that goes far beyond the agony of mortal wounds.

I struggled back from the sea to the shore, staggered by what I had "heard" and seen. Once again, I had been confronted by those rhythmic vibrations—this time not in a controlled situation but in the open sea.

The whales do speak. But why only to me?

Other than a few of the babies and the great white, all were lost in the eight or nine hours we spent on the beach. As each one died, Lambert would rush and mouth-speak how he was paying us a lot of money to save at least one whale. "If you know what is good for you, you will damnwell save one!" When he wasn't threatening us, he was granting interviews to the local media as the resident expert.

The rest of the day and long into the night was a blur of horrors beyond horrors. We took biopsies from all the dead whales before they were pushed into sandy graves dug deep into the shore by heavy, treaded tractors with huge blades. It was obviously an entire pod with young and old alike that had died here this day. Their eyes, glazing over with death, had reflected an obsession among all of them that confused the scientist in me as well as the humanitarian. Why? Why did they want to die? I resolved that if my career had but one purpose I would answer that *why?*

Tired and exhausted, we went back to the marina. I sent Peter home to some much-needed rest, but I continued to fuss about the lab for a time, reluctant to leave the reality of my career in the face of all that I had seen. I wandered into the compound and wound my way back to the main tank where the Orca and the two dolphins were still penned. With an intuitive sense that I wouldn't be dragged back into the water, I quietly climbed the stairs and sat at the edge of the observation platform. Out near the center of the smooth-surfaced pool, three heads effortlessly slipped above water and stared at me, very forlorn.

"Oh, my dear creatures," I signed, "if only you had seen what I have seen on this day, then you would know the true meaning of forlorn." They moved smoothly forward and continued to stare, making no attempt to yank me from my perilous perch. "Do you speak?" I signed. "Did you speak? Was it all my imagination? Were the white whale and the dolphins on the beach my imaginings also?"

The next day and the next, I avoided the main tank wherein lay

my anxieties. Lambert did what he could to make me feel horribly uncomfortable about the events in the pool and at the beaching. He was furious that he had been that close to a true white whale and failed to capture it. At the weekly meeting, he discouraged everyone by announcing that, unless the gate receipts went up immediately, all departments could expect cuts in their respective budgets.

"All of this," he added, overenunciating supposedly for my benefit, "wouldn't have been necessary if the good, soundless Dr. Shar-oon hadn't helped turn the biggest find in marine history, an albino whale, back to the sea. Ten minutes more and we could have had a helicopter there with cables and a sling, and then all of us would have been on Easy Street. But no! Little Miss I-Can-Talk-to-the-Animals let him go."

He sat there at the end of that long conference table, drumming his fingers and giving his infamous, icy stare, which I returned in kind. He then reached down and brought his briefcase up onto the table. "Oh, by the way, Dr. Shar-oon," he spat,

"I have another marine specimen that I need to converse with. Could you talk to this?" He rolled a can of tuna down the full length of the table. "Ask the can if it prefers mayo or mustard with its salad." My face reddened as I saw everyone break into uncomfortable smiles. You don't have to hear laughter to feel it.

Working late on the third day after the beaching, I had to make a firsthand observation of the whale. At the side of the tank, I geared up in my wet suit, scuba tank, and goggles and then climbed the steps to the platform. With some trepidation, I jumped into the water.

All this time, the three creatures sat still and watched my actions. As I hit the water, there was still no reaction. Were they waiting for me to make the first move? Easily said, not so easily done. If you don't know the game, it is very difficult to make any move whatsoever. I kept my head at the surface and readjusted the goggles, then slowly slipped beneath the surface into their world. My eyes adjusted to the crystal blue water and the reflection of the artificial light from above. Their bodies were suspended in the water, yet their heads were floating on the surface. Then in concert, they sank below and hung there, silent-still, staring at me.

What was supposed to have been a simple observation of a new exhibit was taking on a dramatic new dimension. I was waiting for who-knows-what, and they seemed to be waiting for the same thing. Who would speak first, if we were to speak at all? Dr. Lambert was right. All of this was a figment of my imagination . . . a dream.

But if it were a dream, it was my dream, and I would be a fool to let it go to waste. I signed, "Dolphin! Dolphin!"

There was no motion in the water as they floated, their eyes unblinking—no emotion.

I signed again, "Dolphin! Dolphin!" Time slowed, then stopped altogether. Nothing happened. I started to turn away and leave the tank when one of the dolphins moved slightly closer. Suddenly, my inner ear buzzed once again with the delightful, rhythmic pulsations. I *heard*. I *felt*. I knew the word that vibrated in an odd language as old as time. The word, repeated over and over in high modulation, was, "Whale! Whale! Whale!"

It was the language of the sea, but I did not understand. I had signed "dolphin," yet they returned with "whale." It was like I was saying hello and they were saying goodbye. What had I missed? Once again, I felt the pulsation, "Whale! Whale!"

Then, ponderously, wondrously, the whale swam forward, causing me to feel his words. Was this what sound was all about? I was so overjoyed at the rediscovery of communication with these creatures, I almost forgot the wonder of this sensation, which I now must call hearing. There was no other way for me to explain what I felt with respect to this buzzing in my inner ear. The dolphin and the whale sounded—felt—distinct from each other. The dolphin voice was high-pitched and tickled somewhat in communication; the whale, on the other hand, was deep and resonant. The vibrations seemed to soothe and appease.

❀

The beginning, like all beginnings, was rudimentary and primitive. "I am whale, called Dreamer," he sounded. "I have come to the dryside to see what I might see."

I, in turn, signed, "I am sandwalker, called . . ." I paused. His name was rich and reflected an act; my name symbolized nothing. I began again, "I am sandwalker who is sharing with you all that you might want to learn."

"Ah," they toned in unison, "you are Sharing!"

"No! No!" I signed, "I am not Sharing. I am sharing with you . . ."

They again interrupted, "You are Sharing? But you are not Sharing? If you are not Sharing, then who is Sharing?"

Once again, I tried, "I am Sharon who is sharing."

The whale called Dreamer turned his massive head and looked me full in the eye. Regally, he said, "If you are Sharing, then so be it!"

The debate was silly at best and futile. With these marvelous creatures I would share and be called Sharing.

And from that inauspicious introduction, this great captive whale haltingly helped me build my vocabulary and slowly began to relate to me the wonders of the sea. I learned of simple things like the natural foods they ate but never to excess. They ate tuna tails and clacker claws. All were a part of an amazing balance that we, as man, often speak of but rarely attain. I learned more of man, called sandwalker, who walks the dryside. Minute by minute turned to hour after hour. This whale called Dreamer took me by leaps and bounds into a new dimension of understanding and compassion.

I learned that the whales had constructed and committed to memory the history of the world. They called it the Song of the Sea. Bit by tiny bit, I was taught this song. Melody by melody, I learned a philosophy of balance with ALL THAT IS RIGHT IN THE WORLD, their name for a higher being, their God, their great Redeemer. I learned that many of their kind loathed the sandwalker and wished him not only dead but all memory of him washed from the sea and the dryside as well. For the sandwalker kills senselessly.

I was shocked to learn that this whale and the dolphins at the marina had all come voluntarily to places like this. They would be captured intentionally in order to observe the sandwalker in his natural surroundings. They were sent on these missions, which usually ended in death, by whales called the Narwhal of the Horn. These horned, unicornlike whales from the north cast odd spells on those who came to their icy chambers. The Orca had gone there and had heard the singing of the songs of the Narwhal. He then sought to be captured by the sandwalker so that he might add to the knowledge—yet another verse to the Song of the Sea.

The captured ones, both dolphin and whale, stayed with their captors and thrived the best they could in the worst of surroundings. There they entertained and, in turn, were entertained with observations and slow understanding of their great adversary, the sandwalker.

The captive song was built up and passed from whale to whale to dolphin to dolphin. As time passed, one or two of the captives would eventually be returned to the sea, whether by some humanitarian gesture or the simple overcrowding of one marina or another. Then, whether whale or dolphin, the liberated creature would add its song to the great song and carry the new melodies to the Narwhal of the Horn.

As I listened and my comprehension and language developed, I could sense more and more. I was bowled over by the magnitude of their philosophy and their gentle compassion for the spindly-finned creature they called the sandwalker. If the roles were reversed, the sandwalker would plot and plan the death of all who caused him pain. These creatures truly were creatures of spirit and soul. They were and are the embodiment of ALL THAT IS RIGHT IN THE WORLD.

When I had been in the water nearly four hours, I signed, "But why, during the second time that I tried to speak, did you refuse? Why did you lie silent-still, dumb in the water?"

The whale called Dreamer paused for a moment and then slowly began to speak, "We didn't speak because we were mourning a great passing to the end . . . the beginning, and at the same time celebrating a great event, the THOUSAND DEATHS OF THE SANDWALKER.

I shook my head, confused. "What," I waved slowly with my hands, "is the THOUSAND DEATHS OF THE SANDWALKER?"

And Dreamer explained, "It is the death of an entire pod of whales to honor one who has brought greatness to the Song of the Sea. It is a powerful protest as prescribed by the mystic Narwhal, the whale of the ivory horn. Every whale—young, old, male, female—rushes to the dryside, there to die in protest of the horrors the sandwalker has brought to the sea. There, they die to dishonor these creatures who bring sadness to ALL THAT IS RIGHT IN THE WORLD. It is a dying. It is a chorus sung in the last crescendo that washes the sea and even the dryside with its great sacrifice."

"You knew," I signed, incredulous, "of the beaching? You knew of the death of the whales?"

"Yes," he sang, "we knew of the death. In protest and in honor of that which was happening, we could not sing to you. It is only now that the song has settled that we may once again try to teach the sandwalker that which he must know."

My mind reeled with all that logic tried to reject. But I was here, and, for all practical purposes, I was hearing for the first time the history . . . the Song of the Sea. I left the water, for my hands had wrinkled, and I needed time to assess the things I had heard. As I sat there, with my arms drawn about my knees, staring at these three who patiently waited in the water, waiting for my return, one of the security guards happened by.

He mouth-spoke slowly so I could read his lips, "How's it going, Doc? Talked to any more cans of tuna?" He laughed as he walked away. To someone such as this, or for that matter to an intelligent, well-educated person, how do I explain that I, a deaf person, can hear these inexplicable creatures and still be deaf to my own world?

The very same bone, that abnormal growth that caused my deafness, had to be the tuning fork, the vibrating drumhead, that resonated with the fine modulations of the sung word of the whale and dolphin. How long had the sandwalker, in his brilliant ignorance, listened to these wonderful creatures and heard nothing but the echo of his own pride and conceit?

Dried and warmed by the dryside, I slipped back into the water, back to learning . . . the Song of the Sea.

DE

Weeks went by as I learned from the whale. The training tank took on almost a campus atmosphere with the addition of the other three dolphins. With Dreamer and the two dolphins already there, they added bits of knowledge to my understanding.

The staff members constantly teased and taunted me about my obsession and belief in the mammals' ability to communicate. Peter, though, rarely broached the subject, and his smiles seemed more in pity than flirtation. Lambert tolerated my research because the whale seemed to learn the performance routines very quickly.

My life seemed to be wrapped in a slow-motion dream as I absorbed all the whale could teach. But the reality of life at the marina, and especially the opportunism of Dr. Lambert, splashed over me like an ice-water shower. Late one afternoon, I was told quite abruptly not to bother with the whale training. Another dolphin had been isolated in a bay a short way up the coast from the marina; Lambert himself had made the sighting. In spite of federal and state sanctions and his lack of necessary permits, he had snared this new dolphin for his collection.

Not knowing what to expect but having seen Lambert's snaring techniques firsthand, I checked my equipment and stocks of antibiotics. A short time later, Peter excitedly drew me outside near the medical holding pens and urged me to look up. There above us, hanging beneath a hovering helicopter, was a dolphin wrapped in a canvas sling. A wheeled, padded gurney was secured and placed below the descending dolphin. The dolphin finally spun within arm's reach, and, working in the downward blast of the helicopter's rotors, we lashed it to the gurney as the clamps were released.

The dolphin appeared none the worse for wear, but its eyes were opened wide in fear. We wheeled the gurney down the corridor and into the surgery. Lambert appeared moments later, his oily smile showing his feelings of self-satisfaction with the wild capture. "That helicopter," he mouthed, "was an act of pure genius. We had the press following us from the bay like ants following a trail of sugar."

I wildly signed, "Did you ever stop to think that we may not have room for another dolphin? Did you stop to think that there was going to be a furor over the capture of another dolphin without a permit?" My anger was thwarted by Peter who abruptly swung me around. "Come here," he mouth-spoke, "you better see this."

I turned to the examination of the dolphin, and the source of Peter's concern was instantly obvious. The dolphin was very pregnant. As Lambert danced about in glee, celebrating his double capture, I examined the frightened creature who trembled on the gurney. Shots of antibiotic were quickly administered and then a small dose of tranquilizer. I rubbed my hands above her browridge to soothe her anxiety, and then, mercifully, the drug took effect and she slept.

While the dolphin was under the gentle restraint of the drug, I did a complete exam and was shocked to discover that, not only was the baby due at any time, but it was twisted into a breach position. No matter how I twisted it and tried to move the embryonic sac, the child stayed in position. This birth could not be natural. If it had taken place in the wild, the mother and child would have died horrible and agonizing deaths.

Peter confirmed my observations, and, after some discussion, we felt it better to leave her in the observation pen until just before she was ready to give birth. At that time, we would have to perform a cesarean section. As she began to revive from the drug, we moved her back outside and lowered her into the holding pen. I steadied her in the water until she was fully immersed and then left her to awaken and explore her tiny new sea. Observations began immediately, for this would be my first experience with a wild captive birth.

Nothing of any consequence seemed to happen that night, so I slipped away for a time to the whale tank. There in the water, I signed of all that had occurred and of the impending birth. That is the only time I sensed the true outrage of the dolphins and whale at the random capture. "Why can't the sandwalker," the whale sang, "let well enough be enough? Why capture more from the waters of life when more are not needed?"

I tried in vain to explain the need for the sandwalker to understand all the natural things around him. Through capture comes research, I explained, and with research comes better handling of the captured creatures, along with fewer deaths as the result of captivity.

"Yes," the whale whispered in contrasting vibration in my inner ear, "but it would save most of all if you left us all in the wild. We who want to stay and are already captured should be plenty enough for observation. No, my thin-finned friend, the sandwalker likes to possess things—alive or otherwise— just for the sake of possession." With that rebuff, he swam to the other end of the tank, leaving me feeling very alone. It was with shock several days later I discovered the pregnant female had been moved from the smaller medical pen to the larger whale pen. They floated in the water—the five older dolphins, the whale, and the mother-to-be. I'm sure they were exchanging horror stories of capture and captivity.

I stormed and fussed about, finally finding Lambert as he watched throngs of paying patrons milling about and looking expectantly into the tank. "Who gave you permission to mix the new female with performance animals?" I monotoned in mouth-speak. "She is quarantined, Dr. Lambert, because she is about to give birth and needs to be observed."

"First off, little missy," he spat icily, continuing all the while to smile and nod at his paying guests, "what better folk to observe a birth than paying folk? Secondly, I don't need permission to do anything around here. I own this little circus, remember?"

"I remember a lot," I shouted, "an awful lot. It is best that *you* remember."

"Oh," he smiled, "you mean the untimely death of that unfortunate Beluga? Well, like many things remembered, that is best forgotten, too. Oh, by the way, my good doctor, have you seen your photos and biopsies lately? I heard tell things like that turn up missing every day. Just when you need them the most, poof! They are gone!" With that, he turned away, chuckling, and waddled along with the crowd.

I blindly rushed to the lab and my office. There I rummaged about through the back of my desk drawers where I had hidden the pictures and the biopsies. I needn't have bothered . . . Lambert was not one to idly boast of a deed not done.

I sat back in my chair, wounded by the fact that my time at the marina could probably be counted in days, maybe hours. On the other hand, I was almost relieved that I was no longer involved in this twisted act of coercion. Good had been done, but at what price to my own conscience! I sat there, listening to the distant shouts and cheers of the audience as they watched the carnival-clown acts performed by the gentlest of philosophers. I didn't know what to do

The crowd's clapping and cheers crescendoed and then subsided; I knew the whale and dolphins would return to their holding pen soon. Slipping into my wet suit, I rushed out, eager to "speak" with my newest charge. As I approached the tank, they seemed to be waiting in anticipation of my visit.

I bravely signed, "Joyful morning. I pray that the song will always be sung."

I then dove into the water to sense their response. The contrast of the dryside to the waters of life shocked me with its crispness. As the water washed over my body, my mind was washed in a refreshing thought: just after the birth, I would free this wild dolphin and her child.

After exchanging pleasantries, I slowly began to sign-speak through the Orca to the new dolphin. At first, she did not understand my speaking nor how I heard them sing the song. But soon she abruptly asked, "When, then, may I leave this place to join my mate? I am with child, and the birthing will be soon. It is my desire to birth in the open sea. How soon? How soon?"

I looked at her, with her gentle way, and patiently began to move my arms slowly to the whale and other dolphins who readily translated for me.

"You shall be set free, if not by all, then by me alone. But you cannot leave yet. You will not be freed until after the baby is born."

"But why not now?" the little mother wailed in frustration, "Why must the child be born here?"

Once again I sign-spoke, "You were examined. The child must be birthed here, for there is something wrong. The child is twisted inside you. If you birth in the open sea, alone, the child will die and so will you."

The dolphin seemed to recoil in fear, much as a sandwalker would do in the same situation. Her initial reaction was followed in short order by an acquiescence, an acceptance of the fact that the child would have to be birthed under my supervision. I liked the pluck of this creature; I felt a camaraderie with her and a compassion for her.

That day and the next, not knowing what Lambert's next move would be, I worked with the little dolphin whom the others called Laughter Ring. Her thirst for knowledge was unquenchable as she consumed the illogic of the sandwalker's history. She seemed quite perplexed by the sandwalker's desire to own parts of the world and to accumulate wealth.

As I worked with her, she, too, began to work with me. Little by little, she began to tell me the snippets of her everyday life. She was born in a place the dolphins call Winsome Bright, a place of loving and birth. It was here that she conceived her child as she was mated for life—wedded, if you would—to her mate, Little Brother. She told me of their odyssey in the sea and of the chance meeting with the great white whale, Harmony. "He touched my life," she vibrated in the water, "as he touched others with his special singing of the Song of the Sea." Her eyes misted as she ruminated, "His song in time will touch all in the sea."

I nearly stopped breathing when she mentioned the great white whale. "I, too, have met a great white whale. I, too, was touched by his passing in the sea." And I told Laughter Ring the story of the beaching—the Thousand Deaths of the Sandwalker.

"We were there," she cried, as the vibration of her words rang like a bell in my inner ear. "That was Harmony, and that was my mate and I who pulled him back to the sea."

As the days went by, she and the Orca, hesitantly at first but with confidence later, told me stories of great wonder, stories I would be hard-pressed to tell others for fear they would think I had gone completely crazy. These were creatures of the sea and part of a complex society. They had a far deeper philosophical connection with reality and the life that spun around than I could even wish for on my most dream-filled nights.

Some days later, as I neared the observation tank and prepared for my daily conversation with Laughter Ring, my path was blocked by Dr. Lambert.

"Well, little missy, I got good news, and I got bad news. Good news is that we captured another one. Odd thing, though, is that this dolphin *wanted* to be captured. Jumped right in the boat. More the merrier, I always say. Once the fish gives birth, we'll sell the mother and this oddball new one and keep the baby. That's the good news. Bad news is that right after the birth I think you'd best pack your bags and move back to the home for the handicapped. You're done, Doctor. Sorry, but I just can't tolerate lippy staff—even if they can't hear. It's real bad for morale. Heh, heh!" With that, he lit the butt of a partially smoked cigar and slithered away.

Looking blankly into the pool, my revulsion turned to excitement as Laughter Ring spun in the tank, twisted by a great spasm. I leaped into the water to examine her. "It has begun," sang the other dolphins. "The child within wants out."

I held her tight as spasm after spasm wracked her tiny frame. "It has passed," she cried in relief, "but the birthing will be within this tide."

"I will go," I signed, "and bring other sandwalkers to help me lift you from the water to take you where we can help."

"No!" she exclaimed. "My child shall be born in the sea, even if it is a sterile sea. There will be no other way!"

I explained that there would be great danger, and that the baby and she could both die, but she refused to be swayed from her decision. Well, there has always got to be a first time, but a cesarean in the water? I rushed to get Peter and my instruments. As I raced down the concrete walkway, I saw splashing and watched a member of the staff try to restrain the newly captured dolphin who was attempting to leap from one tank to another.

I hurried to the end of the holding tank where Laughter Ring was gently surrounded by the others. Slipping into the water, I arranged the equipment at the edge of the pool and signed, "Yet another dolphin has been brought to the ponds. This dolphin is an odd one and . . ."

Before I could continue, her body seemed again to explode with a spasm. Twisting, muscle-tensing pain stiffened her. Then, as quickly as it had come, it was gone, and she relaxed. Moments later, she tensed again, and then again.

"The time comes soon!" she groaned.

"Oh, dear little dolphin," I signed, "I hope we are doing right to stay in the water. We will help, but it will be very difficult and dangerous."

The nervous anticipation and silence that ensued was broken by an incessant hammering at the other end of the pool. The odd dolphin kept throwing itself at the gate.

"What was that?" she sang.

"That," I signed, "was the dolphin I spoke of. He is an odd catch in the fact that he seemed to demand to be caught even though we didn't want to catch him."

Her body twisted in pain, but her eye widened in apparent understanding.

"Quickly," she cried, "let the new dolphin come near. Hurry!"

I reluctantly signed to Peter, who rushed to the end of the tank and fiddled with the gate controls. Even before the gate was completely open, the water at the end of the pool surged, and the new dolphin swam through the opening.

I was rudely bumped out of the way as this interloper smashed his way to Laughter Ring's side. She turned to look at this odd dolphin. "This," she sang as she grimaced in pain, "is the cause of all this agony. This is the father, my mate, Little Brother." With that, she was wracked with a massive spasm and passed out from the pain.

The other dolphins moved Little Brother a safe distance away, and I set to work. After injecting the pregnant dolphin with tranquilizer, I silkily sliced open her abdomen. I worked at a fevered pitch, and suddenly the embryonic sac was revealed with the child inside. The gossamer membrane was breached, and the baby spun wildly through the water. My eyes blurring with tears from the joy and magic of the birth, I quickly sutured the wound. Peter and I carefully suspended Laughter Ring's inert body in a tank-side sling, which allowed her to be suspended in the water and to nurse without fear of drowning.

I then turned myself to the baby who was floating in the water, its tiny snout just above the surface. On close examination, I found that *it* was female. As if to announce her arrival, she gave forth the loudest burst of vibrations I had ever sensed from the very beginning of my new awareness. The vibration, this burst of buzzing, tickled me, and I broke out laughing in joy, in relief, in exuberance at the continuation and the miracle of life itself.

"Giggles," I signed. "If the mother is Laughter Ring, then the child should be called Giggles."

Shortly after the birth, I began to plan the release of this innocent family of dolphins. I would be hard-pressed to free one dolphin, let alone three, and my thoughts naturally led to an accomplice or two. But whom to involve? Involvement meant risking their job and security, also.

❧

My questions of complicity were answered by the old walrus himself, who notified Peter and the two part-time collegiate assistants they would also be let go. "Clean sweep, Shar-oon. Wipe that old dusty blackboard clean as a whistle. Then nobody will be there to blow it . . . if you get my drift." And then, like a bad odor, he, too, drifted away.

I found Peter in the lab, commiserating with the graduate fellows about their abrupt dismissal. I told them what had happened to the Beluga and the evidence I had held so long. I related the coercion as far as it went and the ultimate theft of the specimens and the pictures.

"Sorry, my friends," I signed. "I never intended to get you fired."

"That jellyfish," mouth-spoke Peter, "I'd give my eyeteeth just for the pleasure of watching him being eaten by a shark a teeny-tiny bit at a time."

"Even with that," I signed, "he'd probably charge admission and sell the television rights. I do, however, have an idea that might bite the doctor where he is most sensitive—his wallet."

Peter and the students leaned forward eagerly as he mouthed, "Lead on, MacDuff, we're all ears . . . or rather eyes."

I began to sign, explaining my half-hatched plan regarding the liberation of the dolphins. It was my simple plan to load them, using the sling, onto the marina flatbed truck and take them down to the wharf. There, we could lower them into two marina boats that were always docked there. Peter and I could then ferry them back to the cove where Laughter Ring had been captured. There, they would have the best chance to rejoin a pod. Our conspiracy was nearly nipped in the bud with the interruption of Dr. Lambert himself.

Surprisingly, he wasn't curious about the four people he had just fired having an impromptu meeting in the lab. Instead, he was nearly frothing at the mouth in excitement. "You wouldn't believe it!" he splattered, saliva flying. "Less than a mile from the coast, there's a veritable parade of dolphins and whales moving north. All the major networks are calling me, looking for background. Hot dog! You've all just been unfired. We are going to go catch a few whales and half a dozen dolphins. I've got orders from two marinas on the East Coast, and the phone's ringing off the wall. Big bucks! Big bucks! Peter, take the flatbed and be down at the docks in an hour. Dr. Shar-oon, you stay here and watch for flying fish."

As Lambert turned on his heel, Peter rolled his eyes in disgust and said, "What do you suppose he means by 'a parade of dolphins and whales'? I've got a friend at the Coast Guard station near Santa Barbara. I'm going to give him a call."

Peter went to the phone, talked excitedly for a bit, and then hung up. "He says it's the darndest thing. There are hundreds of whales and dolphins moving slowly up the coast to the north. They have never seen anything like it."

"Let's worry about this oddity of nature later," I signed quickly. "For now, this will be a great cover to get our dolphins out of here and back to the sea." We rushed about, gathering the necessary supplies: tubes of ointment to protect their delicate skin from the sun and neoprene wraps to hold the moisture close to their skins.

"That," I signed, "was the dolphin I spoke of. He
is an odd catch in the fact that he seemed to demand to
be caught even though we didn't want to catch him."

The flatbed was pulled in beside the tank, and I leaped into the water to explain what was to happen. I then left Laughter Ring and her family with the older dolphins and the Orca to say their goodbyes. I felt an odd thing as I left the water, one word whispered in vibration, "Conclave!" I made a mental note to ask Laughter Ring later about the word and its meaning.

Using the sling and the portable hand crane, we lifted Little Brother, Giggles, and Laughter Ring onto the flatbed truck. Peter and I rode in the bed of the truck with our precious cargo as we began the slow, perilous journey through busy streets to the wharf and the open sea. I sloshed water on their backs trying to soothe their anxiety about the trip. They seemed to take all of it well, and, rather than being anxious or concerned, they reveled in this eclectic collection of sandwalkers.

Being out of the water left me at the distinct disadvantage of not being able to "hear" or "feel" their vibrations as they spoke. It was with great shock that, after I signed to Giggles, "Don't worry, my little one; everything is going to be okay," she responded. I felt the sensation, "What means okay?"

I shook my head in disbelief, and she sounded again, "We swim soon? Waters of life, soon?" Albeit faint and without the positive vibration of being in the water, it was mind-speak. I could feel the sound. I signed to Little Brother, asking him to speak to me, and he responded, "What do you wish me to speak? A song or silly syllables to break you into gales of laughter?" His eyes twinkled as a tear streaked slowly down my cheek.

Peter looked at me oddly but continued his ministrations. I still didn't know if he truly believed in that odd ability of mine to sense these conversations with the dolphins and the whale.

The truck brakes squealed as we stopped for the final time at the end of the long wharf.

Using the small sling that the marina maintained for just this purpose, we lowered all three of the creatures into the Zodiac Bay boats—Little Brother, the largest, into the boat Peter would pilot; the mother and child into mine.

Once the boats were loaded, Peter cast the mooring lines free, and we carefully moved the little boats out into the harbor. I threaded through the congestion of fishing and other marina boats tied to the dock, and, with some odd stares from the deckhands, I moved out into the sea. The staring made me nervous, but it was a rare sight indeed when captive mammals were being taken *out* to sea, rather than being brought *in*.

We rounded the point, and, although there was a bit of action from the waves, the little boats handled it well, and we surged ahead. The fear of being caught was replaced by the exhilaration that can be found only in the biting, saltwater snap of an ocean-borne breeze. I scanned the horizon, looking for the mysterious migration of whale and dolphin. All I

saw were the unmistakable antenna whips of a fleet of fishing boats, working the banks just outside the harbor.

Occasionally, as Peter and I raced the boats along, I could see Little Brother arching himself up to look over the gunwales of the rubber boat. He, too, seemed exhilarated by the entire event. Laughter Ring and Giggles looked small and so defenseless as they lay in their sling blankets. How often had I taken pride during my college expedition days when we captured all sorts of dolphins and seals. What fear they must have felt, being carried away from their homes to be experimented on by the superior beast—he who walks the dryside and cannot sing the Song of the Sea.

As we followed the shoreline, it wasn't long before we brought the boats into a broad and sweeping bay. This was where Laughter Ring was originally captured. Here, she and her family would find their way to the open sea and a pod of dolphin to join in community. I shut the engine off, and the humming vibration stopped, a soundless person's reflection of silence.

With both boats rocking gently in the protected waters, Peter lifted and rolled Little Brother into the inky waters. I groaned with exertion and slowly rolled Laughter Ring over the side of my boat—carefully, for I still feared injury from the surgery. But she seemed as hale and hearty as could be. With the two parents waiting expectantly, I picked up a now-squirming Giggles. As I prepared to slip her gently into the water, she twisted out of my grasp and plopped into the water with all the grace of a rock. None the worse for wear, she swam around in tight little circles, delighted at the sensation of her baptism in the open sea.

I slid over the side of the boat into the cold, biting waters to be closer to my friends. I needed to feel for the last time the brightness of Laughter Ring, this very special dolphin. "You will be well," I signed slowly in the murkier waters of the non-sterile sea. "Your wound of childbirth will soon be completely healed, and you should have no complications.

"Thank you," she stammered, not knowing what else to say.

Small tears squeezed from my eyes and joined the waters from which they had come. "Stay in this cove until you are acclimated with the sea once again," I continued. "Giggles will grow stronger every day. You have no reason to fear for her."

There was a long, painful pause, and then Laughter Ring blurted, "Oh, Sharing, we will miss you so, but we must now join the others of our kind."

I climbed back into the shell and, after staring for some time, turned the little boat to float off, back to the dryside. Peter moved in tandem until we reached the edge of the bay. There, I turned the boat and again shut the engine off—wanting to somehow ensure their safety just by being near. I signed to Peter that I wanted to watch for a time and make sure they were adjusting well. He, too, sat back in his boat and watched in wonder.

In the distance, we could see Little Brother breach high out of the water and powerfully swim away. Like a dutiful father, he returned a short time later, a large fish clamped in his jaws. Then, as before, he dove and swam away again. I saw a small fishing boat cruising from the other end of the bay and continued to watch without concern as Little Brother swam very close to the strange boat. Suddenly, Little Brother turned quickly, leaping from the water and swimming rapidly away from the new boat. The fisherman rose in the bow and, to my shock, lifted a rifle to his shoulder and fired a shot that easily struck the fleeing dolphin.

I sat there in the boat, numbed, shocked into inaction. I looked at Peter in horror and signed, "Why would a fisherman shoot a dolphin?"

"That's no fisherman," he mouth-spoke angrily. "That's Lambert!"

I snapped my head back to the scene and realized that Peter was right. It was Lambert, and he wasn't shooting a regular rifle; he was shooting a dart gun. Without thought, I fired up the engine of the little Zodiac, and, like giving a horse its head, I raced back into the bay. Lambert moved closer to the now-still Little Brother and was preparing to shoot again when he heard my engine racing toward him. I could see the greasy smile on his face as he recognized me and waved. "Come on, Shar-oon," he mouth-spoke, "I got this one and there are two more over there." With that, he drew the rifle back to his cheek.

He was just preparing to fire a second dart into the motionless form floating in the water when he realized I wasn't slowing down. With the wind snapping the tears from my eyes, I slammed the accelerator full forward, and the little Zodiac shot across the flat bay like a drop of water on a hot skillet. My boat hit the side of Lambert's, and my rubber bow caught him full in the chest and smashed him into the water.

Knowing Lambert was temporarily incapacitated, I rushed to the inert form of Little Brother. I killed the engine, and, grabbing a syringe from my kit, I leaped into the water at the same time Laughter Ring and Giggles arrived. Cradling his head, I gave Little Brother a shot that would neutralize the tranquilizer.

"I can't believe it," Laughter Ring cried. "He died seeking to cheer me up with fresh fish. Oh, that silly fool! I loved him so, and now he's dead."

"Not quite," I thought to myself.

Little Brother's eyes snapped open, and he asked simply, "Am I dead?"

"No, my little friend," I signed, "you were only stunned."

"My dear friend," Laughter Ring asked incredulously, "you would attack one of your own to save a life in the sea?"

"Yes," I signed. "Someday man must learn he does not hold dominion over living things. He must learn life is to be cherished with the laws of Nature.

Laughter Ring paused and looked at me queerly. Then, haltingly, she began, "There is much that we have not told you. The dolphin and whale who wait for you in the sterile ponds came to you, not by capture, but out of their own choice. As you learn from them, so do they learn from you. All this knowledge has been passed to a whale or a dolphin that was to be set free. Once freed, they carried this bit of song to the mysterious Narwhal in the colder waters."

"And there is even more," she continued. "Something wondrous is about to occur—a conclave of all the singing creatures in the sea. There has never been such a gathering except at the very beginning when ALL THAT IS RIGHT IN THE WORLD allowed us to be as one."

"You must tell me where the conclave is to take place," I eagerly signed, "for I must see this with my own eyes and feel the song as it is truly sung by all who can sing. Please tell me. I must know."

"Wait, Sharing, you must know the reason for the gathering. The great white whale, Harmony, has called for the conclave of all, and all are moving up the seas to the colder place where the Narwhal live. Here, the tears of ALL THAT IS RIGHT IN THE WORLD have frozen in time in the Bay of Blue Ice. There shall be enacted a plan to save the seas from the greater evil."

I paused and stared at her, then signed, "But what is the greater evil?"

"The greater evil," she continued, "is you, the sandwalker."

"What is the plan?" I asked.

"I know not," she explained. "Only Harmony knows. I know his plan will call for the end of the lives of all the sandwalkers that walk on the dryside."

"Why do you now tell me of this?" I gently asked. She paused, looking at Little Brother and Giggles who frolicked in the waters of life. "For you are more than a sandwalker. In a small way, you have learned to sing the Song of the Sea. You must come to the conclave, not as an interloper or an unwanted guest. You must come as a singer, for a singer you are."

"I will be there! If I have to crawl, I will be there."

Without another word, they swam away and were gone. It was an odd feeling, but, having felt the Song of the Sea, the ocean was no longer lonely. The sea is, was, and always shall be filled with life and the memory of that song . . . that Song of the Sea. My pledge will be honored: I will find that conclave. I crawled into my boat and, as Peter pulled up alongside, openly wept.

"Don't cry," he mouth-spoke. "Lambert's not dead; I saw him drag himself up on the beach."

I smiled through my tears. "I wouldn't cry for him. I cry now for a song."

When I was composed and assured of the dolphins' safety, we turned back to the open sea. The conclave . . . the Bay of Blue Ice . . . this riddle of location rattled about in my brain as we raced our Zodiacs back to the wharf and the waiting graduate assistants. Peter and I clambered onto the flatbed for the bumpy ride back to the marina. My thoughts reeled around the conclave, as I tried to imagine the repercussions in the scientific world alone.

When we got back, I didn't speak to anyone. I just continued to walk up the street to my house. So distracted was I by the question of the conclave location that not until I opened the front door did I realize Peter had followed me, stride for stride. He gripped my shoulders and spun me around. "Sharon," he mouth-spoke, "what is going on? Why are you in such an all-fired rush to get home?"

"Peter," I signed, "I know you think I'm crazy, but I *have* been talking to the dolphins. In the water of the bay, Laughter Ring told me of something wondrous, something inexplicable in all of science. In all our years of research, we have concentrated on what we could do for the mammals of the sea. It never dawned on us that, if they were intelligent, they might be wondering the same.

"Well, Laughter Ring told me of the reason for the early migration of all those whales and dolphins. The whales have called for a 'conclave,' a gathering of all the singing creatures of the sea. At this conclave they will decide once and for all what to do about mankind."

I paced about the room, my thoughts racing, my hands waving. "Think of it, Peter. They are going to meet to decide our fate. Believe me, they were here before us. They have been good neighbors, and we have repaid their hospitality by annihilating them en masse for their body parts. We have kidnapped their young for our own entertainment, and now they are mad. Now, they are going to get even. And you know what, Peter? I can't blame them, and I am going to be there to watch."

I stormed into the house and attempted to slam the door but was stopped by an irate Haida Indian,

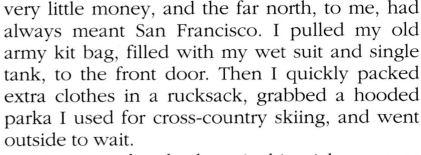

who was still following me. Once again, he turned me forcibly around and mouth-spoke, "Sharon, I don't know if I believe this stuff about talking to animals. But I believe in you. I'll help you."

I shrugged out of his grasp and snapped, "I don't need your help."

"Yes, you do," he answered smugly, too smugly.

"No, I don't."

"Okay, little Miss Doctor, how do you get there? You don't have a car. You have never been out of the state of California. Where is this meeting of the whales anyway, Disneyland? You know where that is. You live in a fantasy land. I am going with you just to make sure you don't get lost. I don't want you to have any excuses to avoid having to eat a bit of crow when we can't find this great meeting. I'll go pack the truck." With that, he slammed out the door. Odd, how easily he got angry. But even angry, he made me smile.

Well, he was right. I didn't have any transportation. I had

very little money, and the far north, to me, had always meant San Francisco. I pulled my old army kit bag, filled with my wet suit and single tank, to the front door. Then I quickly packed extra clothes in a rucksack, grabbed a hooded parka I used for cross-country skiing, and went outside to wait.

Peter was already there in his pick-up, eyes staring straight ahead. In the bed of the truck stood a black Labrador retreiver, steely black eyes staring straight ahead, too, but tail wagging. "What's that?" I signed, indicating the four-legged passenger.

"That's Fred. He goes where I go. He kind of invites himself."

I tossed my gear in back and jumped in the truck. Without a word, Peter accelerated down the street. We careened around the marina and easily entered the steady flow of California traffic.

Feeling like a child being placated by a skeptical parent, I said nothing. The deaf are really good at the game of silence. People who can hear, the listening ones, like nothing better than to listen to themselves chatter. Silence is something they can't stand. I folded my arms across my chest, scrunched down in the seat, and waited for him to break— and break he would.

We drove through Los Angeles and on and on, always heading north. He stopped the truck twice to refuel, once in Bakersfield, and again just north of Sacramento. Oh, he was good! He barely even talked to the station attendants. Fred, the dog, didn't say anything either.

As we were leaving Redding, climbing up beside magnificent Mount Shasta, I felt him say something. I turned quickly, but he had hidden the fact well behind that smirky smile of his. I turned my gaze back to the road, but again I got the feeling that he had spoken.

"What did you say?" I asked sarcastically in mouth-speak, satisfied that in speaking twice he had lost the game.

"I didn't say anything," he enunciated very carefully. "No, Sharon, I am afraid that no matter how you put it . . . you spoke first!"

"I distinctly heard you speak," I snapped indignantly.

"Sharon," he continued patronizingly, "you are deaf, remember? How could you hear me speak?"

"Well, I meant, I felt you speak. I felt you speak first."

"Wrong again, Doc! But let's seek a higher authority. I'll defer to the judge's decision."

I turned back to the road and once again felt him speak. This time I spun around to catch him in the act but found Fred's head inside the sliding back window, barking loudly. As I turned, he pulled his head back outside and stood there, sheepishly wagging his tail. How low will he go? Using a hapless dog to win.

The game over, I asked, "Do you have any idea where we are going?"

"Well," he smiled, "seeing that all the whales were heading north, I thought we would drive that way. North of north is where I come from, remember?" He paused for a moment and then continued wryly, "If I were a whale or a dolphin and I were to have a convention . . . "

"Conclave," I corrected.

"Conclave," he continued. "If I were to have a *conclave* and the *conclave* were to be serious, not one of those 'get together and have a few laughs' *conclaves* but a really serious *conclave,* I'd go to Alaska—the natural conclave place for the discriminating, thinking whale."

Angrily, I snapped my head back around and stared at Mount Shasta wrapped in a cloak of purple sunset. Part of me thought, "May my tongue fall out and my hands cramp if I ever speak to this infuriating human again."

My stoic reverie was broken by a long, wet tongue that slurped across my face. I turned and was eye to eye with a peace-seeking Fred, the dog.

The humor of the situation finally took over, and laughter exploded from me like a bursting balloon. Peter joined me, and we laughed until we cried. With a shaking of my head and a long glance at a proud profile, I finally leaned my head against the cool window and fell fast asleep.

Some time later when it was very dark, I awoke with a start. The truck was idling, and in the green glow of the dashboard light, I could see Peter rubbing his eyes and slapping himself in the face. He flipped on the dome light and looked at me, his eyes haggard and red. "Look, Doc, I've got to sleep for a bit. You drive." He jumped out of the cab and walked around to my side. He opened the door and nearly shoved me under the steering wheel. "We're just outside of Portland, Oregon. Keep the nose pointed north. I'll take over when we get to Seattle." He wrapped his arms tightly around his chest, leaned into the door, and fell asleep.

I turned to the task at hand. Carefully, I gripped the wheel and looked back down the road. There wasn't another vehicle in sight. The freeway was mine, and mine alone. Good! I turned the wheel and pressed down on the accelerator to ease the truck back onto the road, but nothing happened. Silly me! I forgot to put the truck into gear. I pulled the shifter down, and, after bouncing between N and R, I finally settled the indicator on D.

We were off! Now safely on the hard surface of the freeway, we raced on to the north, always north. The night was bright, and the stars were snapping in their brilliance. There is something about driving at night. My only companions were the stars above. My reverie was broken, however, as I was overtaken and passed by a semi the size of Nebraska, which blew by the pick-up as if we were standing still. The pick-up was buffeted by the broken air of the speeding truck, and it was all I could do to maintain control.

That was close! I regained my composure. After assuring myself that no other "maniac" trucks were on the immediate horizon, I concentrated on the tricky road ahead. Well, not horribly tricky—mostly straight—but I had to watch for those casual bends and twists in the road. Half an hour went by, and I felt confident that with no one else on the road I could kick up the speed a notch or two. We were really sailing now.

I hadn't driven at the faster speed for more than ten minutes when, once again, out of nowhere came another maniac semi. With lights flashing, he blasted by me, showing no regard for the safety of anyone else on the road. I had barely caught my breath when I saw another set of headlights in the rearview mirror. Oh, my Lord, another truck?

This truck, fortunately, turned out to be a highway patrolman, who obviously was pursuing the trucks that passed earlier on their death-defying dash up the freeway. I was confused when the patrolman pulled in behind me and turned his red and blue lights on. *They must need me as a witness,* I thought. I carefully pulled over to the side of the road, shut off the engine, and waited. Peter, in the meantime, had

awakened. "What happened? Oh, no," he mouth-spoke as the patrolman walked up to my now-open window, "you're getting a ticket for speeding?"

The patrolman must have spoken when I was reading Peter's lips, for I turned to see him say, "Just keep this pick-up at the speed limit, and we won't have any trouble."

I thanked the officer and sat there feeling a little shaken by the whole experience. Peter got out of the truck and walked back to the patrolman's car. There I could see them yammering away, but, because of the position of the mirror, I couldn't lip-read what they were saying. Peter came back to the driver's side and again slid in.

He didn't say much as he pulled back onto the road. Finally, after a time, he asked, "How fast were you going?"

"I don't know," I mouth-spoke. "Pretty fast. So fast, I didn't dare look down at the speedometer. How fast did the state patrolman say he had me clocked? Boy, if I got stopped for speeding, those truck drivers should get prison sentences for breaking the sound barrier."

As I prepared to slip her gently into the water,
she twisted out of my grasp
and plopped into the water with all the grace of a rock.

"Sharon," Peter began, "I don't know how to explain this to you, but you weren't getting a ticket for speeding. You were going to get a ticket for going too slow. You were doing twenty-five miles per hour. That's not a speed that garners a lot of speeding tickets. How long have you been driving?"

"I don't know. You fell asleep, so I must have driven for an hour or so!"

"No, no, Doc. I mean, how long have you been driving in your lifetime?"

"Oh, I don't know. About an hour or so. Daddy started to teach me, but it just made him crazy, and I really didn't need to have a car anyway."

"You mean," sputtered Peter, reminiscent of Dr. Lambert's spraying speech patterns, "that you don't know how to drive?"

"No, I know how to drive, now. I mean, in the last hour, I learned a lot."

For the rest of the trip, Peter didn't talk much about my close call with the cop. He drove on through Washington, into British Columbia, and up the long, dusty Alcan Highway. He must have been very tired at times, but he never asked me to drive again.

Peter did, however, make an odd observation as we neared the lands where he was raised as a child. We were stopped in the middle of the road, watching a herd of white-tailed deer dance mincingly across the roadway. He said, "The deer were bigger when I was a boy. The bucks, the males, seemed larger, and their racks of horns grander."

"You're right," I signed. "They are smaller."

He looked at me with a cocked eye, "I thought you had never been north of San Francisco. How do you know about the deer up here?"

"Because," I continued, "throughout the world, man hunts the wrong wild creatures for the wrong reasons. We hunt because we feel it's our right to be predator, to be the caretaker of nature. Then, we

hunt the prize—the biggest, the strongest—and with our superior minds and clever weapons, we eliminate the prize from the herd."

"So?" he prompted, as he slipped the truck in gear, and we resumed the bouncy ride.

"So, in nature the tiger, the wolf, the coyote hunt the herds. They balance the great numbers of the antelope and deer, and, in that way, the ones left have plenty to eat and don't starve. But man has removed the predator."

The truck vibrated as the tires kicked up the loose gravel, grabbing for purchase on the shifting road bed. Peter looked at me and politely countered, "Now man has become the predator. Eat or be eaten, the law of nature."

"Not quite," I signed as Peter kept one eye on my hands and the other on the changing road. "Man doesn't hunt like the predators he replaced. The wolf attacks the young, the weak, or the sick, the straggler who isn't as clever as the big bull leading the pack. Man kills the big bull for the prize. Generation by generation, the gene pool gets weaker and weaker, and the deer get smaller and smaller."

Peter became so enthralled by my digital soliloquy that his head was turned full in my direction. "Look out!" I screamed.

My voice brought his head back around, and we narrowly avoided sending the truck straight ahead on a hairpin turn. The truck slid right. Peter brought the wheel around so he was turning with the slide and not against it. Slowly, he regained control, and, in a great boil of dust and rock, we came to a stop.

The dust settled in a swirling mist around us and then suddenly cleared. We were perched high on a mountain curve. Below, the mountain dropped away, and there was the inland Alaskan Ocean, deep green, alive. In the distance, nestled amid trees and pushed against the ocean, was a small town with wharves, docks, and boats all clashing with the velvet spread of Nature's beauty.

We had arrived.

THE EPIC

The sleepy Alaskan fishing village seemed quaint from a distance. But as we drove down the winding gravel road into this little town of Gilroy, Alaska, population 350, we found it had burgeoned into some sort of media mecca, population 500-plus.

It didn't take us long to discover that they were all here for the same reason we were—the great gathering of whales.

"You know, it's odd," I signed as we wound the car through the rushing crush of humanity, "that all these people got here before we did. I didn't see that many cars on the Alcan."

My answer was soon to come. As we parked the truck near the wharf, there came a droning that pervaded the cab and even struck my deadened sense of sound. Sea planes by the tens and twenties floated in the harbor like a flock of ducks preparing to take flight. We could have flown here overnight.

Peter stalked the docks in search of a boat to take us to the Bay of Blue Ice, while I wandered about town with Fred in tow. I eavesdropped from afar with my lipreading. The snippets of conversation I gleaned in my walk were odd: the whales and dolphins were here, with more arriving daily. However they were able, whales and dolphins from the Pacific and from as far away as the Indian and Atlantic oceans had come to the waters of these idyllic bays.

I looked wistfully north and wondered if my friend, Laughter Ring, were there and if she had found the great Harmony. *Come on, Peter,* I thought to myself impatiently. *I need to be there now. I need to hear, to feel the song as it is sung by the master singer himself—the whale who has called this conclave.*

Other bits of sneaked conversation read from afar were a bit disconcerting. Greenpeace and several other conservation splinter groups had joined forces to form an environmental navy. They were patrolling the entrance of the bay to prevent the media boats from interfering with this natural phenomenon. The bay itself was open to the sea, and through these waters paraded this grand procession of all the singing water mammals. They came, and they continued to come, until the waters of the Bay of Blue Ice were frothing with life. They all seemed to be waiting, as were the people who were observing and trying to understand this phenomenon.

The problem of the environmentalists was two-fold. Not only were they keeping the media boats in line, but their own members were curious about this great gathering.

They, too, were forced back every time they tried to venture into the bay. The gentle giants themselves formed a great log boom of living flesh—a floating, impenetrable fence. People were not welcome here, nor were they going to be invited to the festivities.

All of this I related to Peter when he returned, arms loaded with a variety of odd-shaped packages. "Well," he signed, "maybe that's for the best. There's not a boat to be had in the town anyway. The media have them all chartered. I did, however, find a rubber, two-man dinghy at the hardware store."

"Right," I mouth-spoke sarcastically. "And we're going to inflate this little raft with our own lung power and then row the five or six miles up the coast to where first Greenpeace and then the whales are going to let us through?"

"No," he said as he dropped his packages to the ground. "We're going to hike the five or six miles and then, yes, we will inflate the little raft with our lung power and float it into the bay. But we won't have to worry about Greenpeace or the guardian whales at the entrance to the bay. We're going in over the glacier itself. In football, this would be called an end around."

"In the real world, this would be called stupid," I spat. "Let us assume that we get to the glacier on foot. It's three miles long at its shortest point to the sea. I don't know about you, but I don't ski well on millenium-old ice."

"We aren't going to ski," he grinned. "We'll use the boat like a sled. Whooshh! Splash! Right up front in the good seats."

❧

I was doubtful that the plan had any merit, but there was no other. I helped him gather the packages, and we struggled back to the truck. "What about Fred?" I signed as the dog happily wagged his tail, looking from Peter to me expectantly.

"What about Fred?" he retorted. "He's come this far. I'm sure he's ready to go all the way, aren't you, Fred?"

I could feel his bark, and his excitement was contagious. I have done crazier things in my life, but this was getting close to being unique: a Native American, a black Lab, and me—all ice-skating on a glacier.

Having packed, we climbed back into the truck and drove slowly out of town, winding through throngs of people milling about the streets. We followed the road through the little town and to the last vestiges of civilization, where the road itself came to an abrupt end at the trail's head. There, as a form of sandwalker farewell, were several old mattresses, a sofa, some plastic garbage sacks— filled with who-knows-what—and a variety of local newspapers strewn about. I've got to hand it to us humans: if we think we own it, we'll sure use it.

Peter extracted two backpacks from the pick-up and quickly filled them with our gear. I stripped off my parka to enjoy the early morning sunshine that warmed and sweetened the air with the smell of pine and cedar. I started to throw the coat into the truck, but Peter warned, "It's warm now, and it will get warmer later. But, sooner or later, you're going to need that coat."

I bowed, conceding the expert's point. Packed and loaded, Peter placed what felt like the heavier of the two packs on my back. After carefully adjusting my straps to ensure that the load wouldn't slip, he tossed his pack casually over one shoulder. With Fred leading the way, we began our trek to the glacier.

The trail was soft, covered in layer after layer of tree needles and leaves. There was life in the air here, a veritable magic. There is no way to explain the full impact and the wonder of Nature accepted. She owns all, Nature does; people are but passengers on her mysterious journey. Our step quickened as we felt the snap and the thunderous crack of the glacier.

By this time, we had walked three or four miles and my pack seemed a lot heavier; the air, a lot warmer. Eventually, we emerged from the forest onto the broken rocks and chunks of ice that preceded our entry onto the glacier itself, and there we rested for a short time. Peter produced a small camp stove to heat some water, and we had a cup of beef broth and trail mix. I think I know why they call it trail mix, for this batch tasted like it had been mixed with parts of the trail: I think I ate an old shoelace—energy you can tie up and save for later! Fred refused my offerings of a nut or two, instead opting to hunt the neighboring woods. He returned in short order, munching on the remnants of another creature's kill.

"Oh, Fred," I mouth-spoke. "Drop it."

"No," Peter laughed, as he touched my shoulder and turned me toward him. "Dogs are natural scavengers. He will eat what the others don't want, and the others will eat what he doesn't. The parts none of them want will be carted off by the insects or absorbed back into the soil.

Those parts will replace the nutrients removed by the trees, which will be eaten by the squirrels, which will be eaten by the bears and the scavengers to follow. It's balanced. One cleans up after another."

I sat, absorbing this simple lesson I had taught over and over as a teacher's assistant in college. Lessons memorized are not necessarily lessons learned.

By this time, it was midafternoon. I questioned the advisability of attacking the glacier this late in the day. Peter laughed and reminded me that the sun would barely set this June night. This was the night of the summer solstice, the longest day recorded on earth at this northern part of the planet. Satisfied but still cautious, we repacked our gear and garbage and stowed the packs beneath some rocks, taking with us only the bare essentials.

With the rolled-up rubber life raft under his arm, Peter led me onto the glacier. Fred was sniffing behind, probably looking for a cute little snow bunny to eat. Nature has an odd way of balancing beauty with ferocity.

It was difficult to say when we moved from the shifting rocks to the glacier itself. Glaciers are not pristine and clean as one might imagine. One minute we were on rocks and dirt, and the next, we were on rocks and dirt and glacier ice. The outside edge becomes a collector for the slowly moving monstrosity that claws its way across the face of the earth. It has spent lifetimes slowly grinding the earth, molding and moving even mountains.

We angled up and soon entered the smoother ice field itself. Here, over a period of years, the glacier had eroded. I looked up and could see a smooth track of avalanche, where tons and tons of snow had slipped quickly and devastatingly down the glacier. My eyes followed the track down; my breath was taken away by the beauty at our feet.

The Bay of Blue Ice was wrapped in emerald green, tinted by blues so blue that words cannot describe the depth and magic of their color. The ice, as it neared the sea, sparkled with a kaleido-scope of prismatic color and shape. In the bay itself, tiny dots moved about with the tides. I realized that these were not logs; some two or three miles away by ice, but seemingly at our feet, were the whales, dolphins, and flipper-fins. The conclave.

I turned back to Peter. He, too, was caught in this moment. Even Fred sat on the ice and did nothing but look down on this awesome sight. Peter snapped his head around to force himself to the task at hand—inflating the raft. I watched as he huffed and puffed, and slowly the raft began to take shape. It seemed pitifully small in contrast to the glacier now looming monstrously tall.

"Are you sure," I mouth-spoke, "that this is going to work?"

"As sure as I am that my middle name is Abraham," he said confidently. He resumed his blowing, and soon the small raft was totally inflated. He stood back to admire his handiwork. Then, with a flourish, he waved his arm and gallantly motioned that I was to have the place of honor—the front.

I swallowed hard, put my duffel bag in the very front and, after taking a deep breath, stepped into the boat. Peter followed and, placing his legs on either side of me, wrapped his arms around my waist. With one hand, he cumbersomely signed, "Sorry about the intimacy, Doc, but it's a small boat."

I didn't mind. In fact, in a different situation, I might have returned the embrace in kind, but this situation was beyond different, nearing bizarre. I wanted to sit there for a moment, taking it all in and allowing a moment to steel my resolve. But my wishful thinking was for naught as a black bundle of fur leaped into my lap, setting the sled in motion. Fred quickly faced forward, sitting between my legs and the duffel, as we slowly began to slide down the ice. I mouth-spoke loudly so Peter could hear me over the crunching snow and ice, "Your middle name is Abraham?"

"Are you kidding?" he signed, "With a last name of Twofin?" So much for confidence.

Slow became fast became faster became out-of-control, as our rubber toboggan bumped over the ice.

I mouth-spoke back to Peter, "What happens if the glacier doesn't beach with the water? What happens if there is a sheer cliff and a big drop?"

There was life in the air here, a veritable magic.
There is no way to explain the full impact
and the wonder of Nature accepted.

If he answered, I wasn't able to hear anyway, but the answer was soon to come. The raft listed, then turned and spun around so we could behold all those places we had been. We had covered nearly all the distance down the glacier when we spun again and I found the answer to my question. We were airborne!

The boat sailed off the ice like an errant Frisbee and maintained a form of aerodynamics as it spun crazily out over the sea. As quickly as our adventure had begun, it ended. Splashdown! I was thrown forward by the abrupt plunge in the water, but with Fred cushioning my head, I was uninjured. I sat up and looked around.

You did not have to be a hearing person to feel the silence that lay like a blanket over this inlet, this bay. The water was as still as glass and inky in its appearance, although it was very clear. In the water around us were dolphins, whales, flipper-fins, and some other creatures that I never would have thought of as singers of the Song of the Sea.

Peter urgently tapped on my shoulder, and I spun in the tiny boat. His face was as white as a ghost. "What is this?" he mouthed. "What are they all doing here?"

I signed, "So much for 'believing in you.' Peter, this is what I have been talking about. This is the first time since the beginning of time that the conclave has ever been called. It can only be called when a species feels threatened by extinction. It had nearly been called over the extinction of some whales. At one point, the Narwhal of the Horn tried to call a conclave, fearing their own extinction, but never has it actually been called before." I waved my arm around the bay, which was ringed by the blue ice of the glacier and filled to silent-still capacity with thousands of thinking creatures—a veritable seething maelstrom of life.

"This is . . . conclave!"

The whales and the dolphins stared at us with baleful eyes but did nothing. Time seemed to freeze in space as we sat looking at them, and they at us. The impasse was broken when we were rushed from behind by a large Orca, who swam through the satin waters and brushed the boat. His wake caused us to rock precariously, and Fred, still held in my arms, began to bark angrily, warning all to stay back. The hackles on the back of his neck were raised, and I could feel him growl—deep and menacing.

The little boat lay still in the water. Two Orcas swam quickly toward us from opposite directions, tossing our little boat about in the water. The bone in my inner ear began to ring with the vibration of the low tones of one, then two, then ten, then a hundred voices softly chanting together, "Conclave . . . conclave . . . conclave." As suddenly as it had begun, it stopped, and my inner ear was silent once again.

I twisted my head, felt another tingling, and sensed a new sound. This was quieter. I turned this way and that, trying to home in on the vibration.

"What is it?" furtively signed Peter.

I froze him with a wave and tensed again, seeking the source of the sound. It was getting louder. It seemed to be one or two voices intently calling, "Sandwalker. Sandwalker." I spun my head, and there, not fifty feet away, was one of the Orcas that had brushed the boat. He called again, "Sandwalker. Sandwalker."

Then, behind me, I heard another and spun to that sound. He, too, called, "Sandwalker. Sandwalker. He who walks on spindly fins on the dryside. He who holds dominion over the song sung in the sea."

Peter spun me to him, "What is going on? Are we in danger?"

"I don't know. It doesn't sound good. But it's hard to hear clearly without the resonance and the amplification of the water." I turned back around, my brows knit and my head cocked slightly in concentration.

There was a moment of silence, and then, almost in chorus, the other Orca took up the ominous chant, "Sandwalker. Sandwalker. He who left the sea and returns only to kill the others. Sandwalker."

Suddenly a new voice—like ice itself—joined the duet. The sound cut me through to the heart. It was whispered, yet loud. It was sweet, but bitter-sweet. It was an icicle, sharp and deadly. "Sandwalker!" the voice demanded. I spun to the side and gripped Fred for fear he would leap into the water and attack. Not ten feet from the boat was an alabaster-skinned Narwhal of the Horn.

"Sandwalker," he intoned again. "He who came to us in the water in shells. He to whom we tried in vain to teach the Song of the Sea. He who, to reward the song, killed the singer of the song and ripped from his head . . . his horn."

Softly, but with great intensity, the creatures of the conclave chanted in staccato, "This was not good."

The Narwhal continued in his hypnotic, icy tone, "With the bloody horn, the sandwalker killed another, and then he had two horns. He coveted the horns as prize. He did not eat the meat, violating all that is holy in the sea and the simplest rule of ALL THAT IS RIGHT IN THE WORLD."

The water danced with an electricity that snapped blue, silver, and green iridescence just at the surface. In unison, they cried, "And this was not good!"

The two Orcas, overlooked by the chanting of the Narwhal, suddenly charged the little boat again, rocking it perilously. Peter and I grabbed the sides to steady the craft against the wake of these two fleshy torpedoes. Fred snapped his head to and fro, seeking an enemy worthy of his jaws.

A maniacal laugh came from the Narwhal, and then he began again. "We, the Narwhal, were forced to hide. We, the Narwhal, alone carried the message, warning the others of the sand-walker's lack of soul and spirit. We hid in the icy corridors and palaces where our reflections in crystal strengthened our resolve. We sought others to teach them the story. And they came. And they listened. And they changed the Song of the Sea forever."

In powerful harmony, the bay rippled with, "And this was good!"

The vibration stopped, and time seemed to freeze like the blue ice that surrounded this bay of decision and change. "We have died for the sandwalker in a thousand deaths. We have cast ourselves in protest to the dryside, there to become one with the end . . . the beginning. There to rot and demonstrate to the sandwalker that he does not hold dominion over the sea. There to send a message to the sandwalker that we control our own destiny. We can, we will, and we did call upon our own deaths and a return to the end . . . the beginning."

So loud now that my inner ear ached, they chanted, "And this is good!" From this forceful vibration, I could read in Peter's face that he, too, at strong intervals, could hear, although he did not understand what the vibrations meant.

Breaking the stillness, two angry voices, in counterpoint in front and behind, intoned by whispered vibration, "Sandwalker. Sandwalker."

They stopped and then started, "Sandwalker. Sandwalker."

"Sandwalker! Sandwalker!"

Again and again, they started and stopped and stopped and started. The result was terrifying.

I kept turning back and forth as each one, in turn, made its call, "Sandwalker! Sandwalker!" Never in all my life have I been so frightened, for the whispering carried an unspoken mes-sage: "We're coming—we're coming." Peter was watching my face and realized that some-thing was about to happen. It obviously wasn't going to be a matinee at the marina with dol-phins and whales leaping to the delight of the audience.

Abruptly, there was a surge in the water like a bulge, a monstrous ripple moving forward. I looked behind, and there was another doing the same. The two Orcas smashed into the boat and screamed with a force of vibration that chilled my blood and froze me in place.

"Sandwalker!!"

This time, they didn't skim by. This time, the full force of their fury tipped the boat almost onto its side. Try though I might, I could not hold on. Every muscle in my body was frozen by the horrible, intoned death-keen of the Orca. I hit the water, and even the shock of its coldness didn't break the spell. I simply couldn't move. Straight ahead and slightly below me under fifteen feet of water were the two Orcas. Mouths open with long, ivory-colored teeth forming an unconscious smile, they floated, waiting and watching. A moment, an hour, I know not which, went by before I could control myself again.

I had just begun to kick myself to the surface when they intoned again, "Sandwalker—Sandwalker!" The vibrations now unencumbered by the dryside, the force was unbelievable, and again I was frozen.

The sultry vibration of the Narwhal of the Horn called to the Orca, "Take them now, my sweets. Take them now to the end . . . the beginning. Take them to ALL THAT IS RIGHT IN THE WORLD."

A movement in the water caused me to look up, breaking the reverie of the eerie call. What at first

As he pushed me from the water, I had felt
the greatest of all the calls when the two Orcas,
in concert, bellowed their death call, "SANDWALKER!!!!!"

looked like a rippling shadow on the surface turned into the full form of a man leaping headfirst into the water. It was Peter. Surrounded by the silver bubbles of the dryside that followed him on his erratic dive, he saw the Orca first, then turned and spied me. He swam in hard strokes, reached down, and grabbed my swirling hair. With all his might, he flung me to the surface and now was between me and my attackers.

What happened next was simultaneous and confusing. He grabbed me by the back of my now anchor-weight parka and, with herculean strength, threw me into the boat. Still paralyzed but beginning to feel sensation, I lay with my feet stiffly pointing off the side. As he pushed me from the water, I had felt the greatest of all the calls when the two Orcas, in concert, bellowed their death call, "SANDWALKER!!!!!"

Peter, who up to this point had felt a bit of the vibration and its gentle subtleties,

took this one full force. I could feel, even as I was being pushed from the water, that his muscles went slack in response to the death call. I lay there, helpless in the bottom of the boat, trying to will my body back to action, but it was as if I had been severed from my conduit of reality and control. A grating sensation wiped my face from jaw to forehead like wet sandpaper. Over and over again, it ground across my face. It was an anchor of feeling, and I responded slowly to the release of the nerve blockage. I could feel again, and with the feeling came nerve and muscle control. I swung my legs around and sat upright in the boat, dazed by all that had happened.

The swipe of a very rough, wet tongue snapped me back to reality—the bay, the conclave, and Fred, the dog. I hugged him and then remembered how I had come to be in the boat. "Oh, my God! Peter!" I flopped myself around and lay across the round, rubber side of the

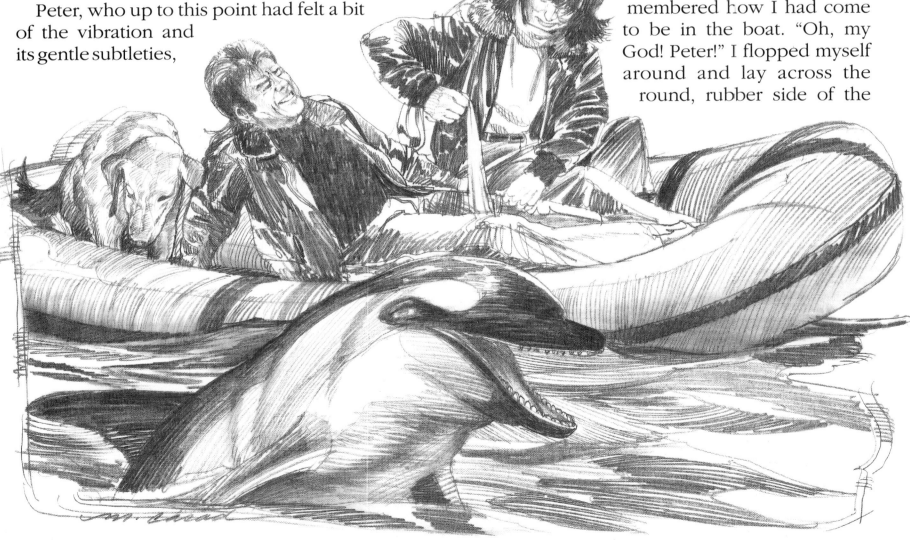

boat. I peered into the crystal waters below. At first, I saw nothing, and then I saw all.

Five feet below the surface, slowly spinning, was Peter, his eyes frozen open by the paralyzing call. Then, almost in slow motion, one of the Orcas turned sideways and grabbed Peter full-mouthed by the hip and thigh. The water swirled in a cloud of pink. I fell back into the boat unable to move, frozen by the horror of watching someone, who just moments before had saved my life, die in my stead. I watched over and over in brief memory flashes as the man I loved but had never told shut his eyes in pain when those powerful jaws of death closed around him.

I lay in the sloshing water on the bottom of the boat, my tears mingling with the waters of life. I couldn't just lie there. Peter deserved a better memorial. I sat up again and looked out over the now-still waters that were misted in a swirling, red cloud.

From nowhere, a form arched from the water like a missile being fired from below. My first thought was that the Orcas were breaching—to fall on the boat and reclaim the other sandwalker for the Song of the Sea. But the form was not an Orca; it was the body of Peter Twofin being thrown from the sea. In a low arc, he flopped into the boat. I was sure he was dead—but this corpse began to cough. He was alive!

As he pulled great gasps of breath into his lungs, I tended to the wounds. I took off my coat and yanked the nylon cord that acted as a drawstring on the hood. I wrapped this around Peter's leg just above the wound in his thigh, twisting it around and around to form a tourniquet and stem the flow of blood. The wound in his hip was more of a deep rent in the skin that appeared superficial, although it probably would need stitches later.

"Well, Doc," he mouth-spoke, "welcome to the Marineland of the Northern Pacific! Home of dolphins and whales who will bring you tears of joy that will rip your heart out. Literally." He laughed, then winced as I twisted the tourniquet tight.

He looked at me oddly, "How did I get out of the water? Last thing I remember is feeling like a frozen filet of cod, and then suddenly I am flying back into the boat."

Almost in answer, a form threw itself at the side of the boat. The whales were back! I lay down beside Peter to better view what seemed to be the final attack.

Once again, there came a bumping on the bottom of the boat when a form threw itself at the side. This time, it breached and landed up on the gunwale. The rubber-sided boat crumpled under the weight. We were looking into the low-angled sun, and, for a moment, we were blinded by the contrast of brilliant light and silhouette.

A voice vibrated in my inner ear: a good voice, a welcome voice, a sweet voice . . . the voice of Laughter Ring.

One form was joined by another as Little Brother, too, plopped himself on the edge of the boat. Even Fred seemed to understand that these two odd creatures were friends. "Sorry we were late!" laughed Little Brother. "Fortunately, we got here in time for the main course. In this case, coming just for dessert would have been a disaster."

I translated for Peter as Laughter Ring chided her mate for his tasteless remarks. Peter laughed and then grabbed his side, wracked with pain from his injuries. Sitting there, it suddenly dawned on him that the dolphin had indeed been speaking and, with sign, I had been talking back.

"They do talk!" he croaked in mouth-speak. "And you talk to them."

"Well, score another point for belief and believing," I signed in mock indignation. "You thought I was making this all up?"

Peter grinned sheepishly, "So, what happens now?"

I turned back to Laughter Ring. "What is happening now?" I signed.

"There is a great debate raging beneath us even as we speak," she toned. "Harmony called the conclave, but the Narwhal of the Horn are trying to establish rules to ensure their control. Harmony is wise to the Narwhal's twisted sense of fair play and, with our help, has created his own alliance with the blues, the humpbacks, and the dolphins. He had enough to control the conclave with the support of the dolphins alone, but he felt he needed a mandate. The decisions here will be hard, and the results far-reaching."

I paused to digest the fact that politics was universal in our world of twisting values and philosophies. "You say the decisions will be far-reaching. Far-reaching to what extent and to whom?" I asked tentatively, sure that I already knew the answer.

Laughter Ring turned her eyes downward and vibrantly toned, "For eternity, the decision will affect the sandwalker and all his children's children's children."

"Then I claim the right to speak for the sandwalker and to sing his defense." I gambled that somewhere in the Song of the Sea was a rule or value that allowed the accused to present his own case. I sat in the boat defiantly, feeling like a drowned rat.

Little Brother turned to Laughter Ring and said, "I do not know the song that well, but I will take her message to Harmony if he wins the mandate. If not, I will have to put the question to the Narwhal of the Horn."

❦

Though it was very late in the day, the sun still burned in the sky, adding a twisted, dreamlike quality to an already crazy day. As we waited, the sun dried our clothes, and the chills dissipated. In fifteen-minute intervals, I opened the tourniquet on Peter's leg, allowing the blood to circulate in hopes of avoiding complications. The waters around us teemed with life; the sea snapped with anticipation. Every so often, Little Brother or Laughter Ring would slip off the side of the boat to seek news of the debate. Each time, they returned shaking their heads in dismay.

Nearly an hour later, Laughter Ring again went to seek news. It wasn't but a minute before she leaped back to the boat. "Harmony will have his way. The Narwhal of the Horn are very angry. Godwin the Avenger, their choirmaster, proclaimed the conclave cancelled and urged all to leave, but none would. Now, they are bound by the conclave and its great import. The Narwhal have remained, but they are dangerous still, very dangerous. Watch them."

"But what of my demand for defense?" I waved angrily, caring not for the petty political dissent.

Laughter Ring paused, "At first, Harmony said, 'No!' and dove to the deep. Moments later, he rose and acquiesced. No matter his prejudice, he is honor-bound by his duty to the Song of the Sea.

"For, you see, many, many tides ago, he was a scribe, a dispassionate recorder of the song. His pod, an old, old group of Great Whale with a song nearly as old as the Song of the Sea itself, died the THOUSAND DEATHS OF THE SANDWALKER. With that death came the death of his greatest love and his greatest enemy. He believes the sandwalker killed his family, his friends, his enemy—if not by deed, then by intent. He was lost without them and tried also to cast himself upon the dryside to die in protest. The Song of the Sea echoes within his empty soul, and his blood is on fire as he seeks the final answer to the final question. He has now proclaimed you the leader of the sandwalker . . . the symbol of all the dryside near this sea and throughout the drysides all over the world."

Behind him in a cathedral setting
floated a wall of dolphins, flipper-fins, and whales.

In relief, I laughed; but in anxiety, I signed, "Ah, I have just been made queen of the dryside earth."

Laughter Ring shook her head gravely, "This is no laughing matter. What happens here will reach far into the future, for all the tides that remain in the waters of life. Here, you will speak for the sandwalker. You will be the first to hear the decision. You will be the first to suffer the punishment if indeed punishment is rendered."

Sobered by her comments, I explained to Peter what was to happen. Moving Fred from atop my duffel bag where he had made an impromptu bed, I spread out and checked my equipment. Peter politely turned his back to check the oxygen level in my single

tank while I quickly slipped into my wet suit. With the multiple layers of the suit, even the cold waters of this northern inlet wouldn't bother me for a while. Long before hypothermia could set in, I would be out of air. Long before I froze, the conclave would have decided. Geared up, Peter strapped the tank to my back. I asked Laughter Ring, who was now in the water with Little Brother, where I would meet the great Harmony.

"That," toned the dolphin, "I don't know. Harmony will send for you, I guess. There has never been such a . . ."

Her comments were cut off as the world seemed to explode right before us. Like a geyser gone mad, the water first twisted and boiled, sucking into itself, then shot into the air. Out of this foam and froth breached the most powerful form I have ever seen. Against the backdrop of the never-dying summer sun was the great white whale . . . Harmony. He appeared to stand on his tail some eight meters above us and was so close I could touch his pearly, opalescent skin.

In contrast to the explosive breach, he crushed softly back into the

sea. I could hear the mighty vibration in my inner ear as he toned loudly, "Tell the spindly-finned sand-walker, my sweet dolphin friends, that Harmony will speak to *it* now!"

With shaking hands, I pulled the mask over my face and bit down hard on the mouthpiece, my source of life-giving oxygen. Holding the face plate, I leaped into the sea. Though the suit insulated me, it still seemed an icy shock to slip into those waters. I dropped down and down as I gained my bearings. I spun around, weightless in nearly twenty feet of water. There before me, suspended in the crystal waters of life with shafts of sunlight forming a curtained background, was Harmony. His tail and fins moved effortlessly, keeping him exacting still in the water. I, on the other hand, had to wave my arms and legs wildly in an attempt to maintain buoyancy and position. Behind him in a cathedral setting floated a wall of dolphins, flipper-fins, and whales.

The water vibrated with snaps and buzzes of language as Little Brother explained to Harmony that I could hear the song and that he could speak to me directly.

He seemed unimpressed and unmoved as he angrily sang, "You say she can hear our song? After all of eternity, there now is one sandwalker who has bothered to listen? To see if we sing? To see if we think? To see if we feel?"

Floating in the water, I listened as this great whale sang his powerful accusations. "We have reached out to the sandwalker since the beginning of time," he continued. "We offered our song to him and have been rewarded with death. We have welcomed him to our seas, and he has turned the seas sour with his greed and our regret. We have offered the laughter of the dolphin, and the sandwalker has ripped him from the sea in odd kelp weavings. We have offered to the

sandwalker the whale and his singing of the song, and we have received in return an audience that refused to listen and opted instead to devour the choir."

In the distance, I could hear the insistent, hypnotic whispering of the Narwhal, Godwin, "This is good! This is good! Kill the sandwalker! Kill the sandwalker!" Faintly, others echoed the chant, the Narwhal sentiment, but no verdict had yet been reached.

Harmony, disregarding the Narwhal, continued his song, "The dolphins, Laughter Ring and Little Brother, have brought to us great tales of the ability of the sandwalker, and now, for the first time, they bring one to hear the song. After all that has transpired since the beginning of time and from the first tide that rolled from an otherwise still sea, the sandwalker has decided that maybe this is the tide to reach out to his brethren. This is the tide to sing the Song of the Sea."

From afar came the piercing whisper of the Narwhal, "No! No! No! Not true! Not true!"

Harmony paused, turning slowly in the water, tail slightly down. The light cast from above drove a silvery spike shimmering through the water. The last vestiges of his song echoed off into the distance. He then continued, "Well, the sandwalker is here. This sandwalker has appeared in the defense of all the sandwalkers. Hear me, all who live in the sea and sing the song. The sandwalker has defiled the sea for the final time. The sandwalker has killed the last creature of song for sport, not to eat the meat, but to let it lie fallow and rot in the sea, violating all that is holy. The conclave sings now and will cast their lots. My ruling is, and I ask for your voice . . . the sandwalker should die, his death to be allowed as prescribed by ALL THAT IS RIGHT IN THE WORLD and recorded by the Song of the Sea!"

The silence was stunning. In the distance, like lightning crackling down a copper wire, came the delighted, static whispering of the Narwhal of the Horn, "Yes! Yes! Yes!"

❧

Before the proclamation could be mandated by all that moved in the conclave, I signed to Laughter Ring, who translated, "No! I have the right to sing the song. I have the right to offer defense. I call upon my right. By all that is holy, let me sing!"

The little dolphin's voice vibrated loud and true in the crystal, still waters. Harmony, who had turned away during the passion of his proclamation, slowly focused his attention back on me. He nodded his head in a quizzical movement, "She said that? I heard nothing. Yet, dolphin, you say she has called for the right to sing the song? What proof have you that this is not some silliness, a jest at a very inopportune time? I warn you this is not a time of laughter, dolphin, and—friend or not—your lot can be cast with those you support."

I signed again, "Watch my hands, my arms, all of my body. I cannot sing out loud. I have not the voice and could not hear it if I did. So instead, I sing with all of me, but, still and all, the song is sung. Please listen and watch as I try to explain the evil and wrong that has been committed against all that live in the sea and all that live on the dryside, too!"

Harmony had moved closer and closer as I signed. He listened as word after word was instantly translated and broadcast into the sea.

"We were wrong," I signed. "We have done monstrous evil in ignorance of our action. For greed alone, we have destroyed that which was never ours to own, but only to borrow. For Earth belongs to Tomorrow. If Earth is the gift and Tomorrow the receiver, then we give nothing. For we are destroying the gift itself."

"Stop!" roared Harmony in a tone so heavy with vibration that my head wanted to explode. "Don't speak in riddles! Don't play games with the song as it is being sung! Do not, sandwalker, mock us!"

I sucked in a large gasp of the canned air to still my pounding heart and continued, "I do not mock the song. I play no games. I, a sandwalker, am here to plead our case. We, the sandwalker, are guilty!"

Closing in, the Narwhal's whisper scraped like a knife on a rock. "Ohhh, yesss! Yes! Yes!"

The waters echoed silent-still. No movement. For a moment, there seemed to be no other life than mine, isolated and alone in the presence of ALL THAT IS RIGHT IN THE WORLD. Then my body tingled as a thousand voices spoke at once—a cacophony of sound and vibration.

"What?" roared Harmony in disbelief. The waters once again settled into silence. "You come here to us and admit guilt. Should I not then place my verdict at the sandwalker leader before me? Should I not taste blood as the sandwalker has tasted the blood of my family, my friends?" The great whale began to move closer in the passion of the moment.

"Should I not, little puny-finned one, bite down once on that head of yours and thereby silence the only sandwalker witness to the Song of the Sea?"

Tensely, like a plucked string on a violin, Godwin twanged gleefully, "Do it! Do it!"

"Silence!" toned Harmony forcefully. All again was quiet-still. "You plead guilty?"

"Yes," I signed.

Calmed now and curious, Harmony continued, "Answer these questions—some of personal curiosity, others of a philosophical nature. Will you answer them from the heart for all sandwalkers?"

"I will," I signed solemnly. Laughter Ring and Little Brother translated my movements into the

Full he breached from the sea, and full he fell
on Godwin. The fiery eyes of the Narwhal went blank
as his back broke . . . he was dead.

words sung to Harmony. Although he did not understand all of my movements and signing to begin with, he began to understand a little and then more and more. Out of deference to his friendship with the dolphins, he allowed them to continue to translate, although they probably were not needed.

Harmony studied me. His eyes were deep, etched round with lines of memory, memory of sights he had seen and the song he carried in his soul. He paused and rose slowly to the surface to vent and then, after a brief time, settled down into the water until his buoyancy matched mine, and we were once again eye-to-eye.

"In the sea," he sang, "we have the sharp-fin, a natural predator to all except us and, at times, even to our weaker members. But that is the mandate of ALL THAT IS RIGHT IN THE WORLD. On the dryside, do you have predators?"

"We have."

"What are they?" he asked quietly.

"We have creatures called bears, lions, tigers, wolves, and coyotes. We have eagles and hawks that soar above the dryside on feathered wings."

"Do these predators prey on the sandwalker?"

I paused. There was no need for deception; I had already pleaded guilty. "They did, but we vanquished them. For the most part, they are all gone. We have killed many of them."

"What, then, preys on the sandwalker? What is the balance point on the dryside? Are there natural things, or do all sandwalkers survive?"

"We are eliminating disease, the balance point, the natural predator. Nature herself, often called All That Is Right in the World in the Song of the Sea, is being vanquished."

"Do you wish to live forever?"

"No!" I answered, confident of my personal beliefs on mortality.

"Does the sandwalker wish to live forever?"

I sighed and then signed, "Yes."

"In the Song of the Sea," he sang in beautiful, rich vibration, "it is sung that in the beginning we who live in the sea were to go forth and multiply, balanced by ALL THAT IS RIGHT IN THE WORLD. If the young, old, or infirm were meant to live, they would live. If they were meant to die, they would incorporate with the end . . . the beginning. In that way, nothing would ever die. Death honors the living, and the living honor the dead. But the sandwalker multiplies and multiplies and multiplies. Where will he go when he has no more flat land dryside?"

My mind raced, seeking answers to an enigma. Man indeed survives. "He will have nowhere to go but to the mountains."

"And when the mountains are filled?"

"To the deserts," I answered.

"And when they are filled?"

I paused and then slowly signed, "To the sea."

Harmony floated there before me. The water was flat, and, for a moment, the tides froze. There was no movement from any of the whales, dolphins, or flipper-fins. In a majestic tone, Harmony began to sing. "The sandwalker is guilty by action. The sandwalker is guilty by deed. The sandwalker is guilty in the pleadings of this leader, Sharing. Therefore, he is guilty. How does the conclave vote?"

In somber tones like the keening of a bell, the conclave rang out in unison, "Guilty!"

In the not-far distance, I could feel the tinkling laughter of Godwin, "Yes! Oh, yes! Yes! Yes!"

Harmony sighed as he released a mercury-colored balloon of air into the sea. It coalesced and twisted around in pursuit of the dryside and freedom.

"The sandwalker is guilty. Therefore, he is now condemned!" He paused. "Go forth!" he cried to the conclave. "Go forth and hide. Go to the deepest of the deep and wait. In time, the sandwalker will destroy himself. In a short time, he will kill all on the dryside, himself included. He will crowd himself to the sea. With nowhere to go and with nothing to eat, he will turn on himself and, like the sea snake that thinks his tail another snake, will devour himself. Then, and only then, will the song be sacred again. Then, and only then, will the waters of life be sweetened by ALL THAT IS RIGHT IN THE WORLD."

Harmony, with all the grandeur of his countenance, turned in the water and slowly swam from view. The conclave now broken, all the whales, dolphins, and flipper-fins began to disperse. I turned to Laughter Ring and Little Brother. "What does it mean?" I signed, relieved that, for the moment, I was still alive.

"It means," toned Little Brother morosely, "that it is over."

"I . . . I don't understand what Harmony meant. What is the punishment? We are just to be left alone?"

Laughter Ring answered, "Yes, you are to be left alone. Without the interference of the love or consciousness of the sea, or of ALL THAT IS RIGHT IN THE WORLD, the sandwalker will die."

They were right. The human race was on course to destroy itself. The conclave had merely sealed the

fate already self-delivered. Their answer was to do nothing but wait and hide, knowing that the sandwalker's greed and supreme desire for immortality would be his demise. Harmony was right: the sandwalker was damned by his own desires. "Is there nothing I can do?"

In unison, they shook their heads and sang, "Nothing." The somberness of the moment was broken by the torpedolike return of the dolphin-child, Giggles. She swam around and around, pleased to see me and happier still to be reunited with her parents.

"I must go to Peter," I signed, "and tell him of all that has happened." I rose in the water toward the light of the nighttime summer sun.

As I neared the surface, I heard a twisted whisper, "Not so fast, little dryside sister!" In the distance, I could see the ghostly outline of a Narwhal of the Horn, his ivory tusk waving defiantly in the crystal waters.

"Yes! Yes! Yes! The conclave is over for all save you. It is not as easy as Harmony decreed. We need blood in the water to seal the fate. We need your blood, sandwalker. For you know the song, and it must not be sung to the others . . . the sandwalker. He might learn to listen. He might change his way."

Godwin swam closer and closer, his horn dancing back and forth, reflecting bits of light that shot errantly all about. "Yesss, you will die now!" With that, he surged forward, his horn lowered like a lance, and slashed by. At first, I was relieved that it had been a clean miss and spun to face him again. So sharp was his horn that, were it not for the water turning to a pink cloud, I would not have known that I was injured. On my right shoulder was a gash that cut through the multiple layers of the wet suit and into the flesh.

Again and again, he sliced by me in the water, each time cutting a bit more.

"This is good!" he chanted over and over and over. "This is good!"

Desperately, I forced myself to swim up and away from the demented Narwhal and finally broke to the surface, where strong hands grabbed me, lofting me into the boat. I had seven lacerations like fine razor cuts over my abdomen, legs, and arms. Peter ripped the goggles from my face, and I breathed deep of the sweet-scented air of the dryside. Relieved it was over and safe in his arms, I pulled the hood back and shook my hair free, my heart pounding. Momentarily, I felt safe.

Suddenly, an iridescent horn lanced through the bottom of the boat. Fred, finally confronted with an attacker, closed his strong jaws around this bit of bone—this lethal dagger. The shock of not being able to readily pull free caused Godwin to breach, elevating the boat like an airborne pancake. Only then did Fred reluctantly let go, and the whale allowed us to fall back to the surface.

We sat in the water, spinning around. "What was that?" mouth-shouted Peter.

"That was part of the conclave," I signed wildly, looking about for the next attack. Once again, it came from below as the horn erupted through the bottom of the boat. Again and again, it slashed, seeking solace in attempting to pierce flesh. Knowing that there was no recourse, yet not fearing death, I turned to Peter and signed, "The odds are we won't survive this." With that, I put my arms around him and kissed him full on the mouth. I refused to die with any regrets, and I would never regret that kiss.

Our embrace was broken apart as the horn shafted between us and then retracted for its next assault. But the attack was cut short by a monstrous breaching right beside the boat. The air vibrated with challenge, and I could hear Harmony's call of anger. "Back off, Godwin of the Narwhal. The conclave spoke. The verdict was to let them be."

"No," whisper-whined the horned whale. "She knows of the song. If she sings it to others, they will save themselves from their earned fate. She must die now, white whale, and if you interfere, you will die, too." With that, he turned back to us and lowered the horn.

Chastised, Harmony settled below the water. The Narwhal slashed his horn back and forth, causing the sea to foam and boil in turmoil. "Now, you die! Now, you die!" he whisper-screamed. Lying full on the surface, he began the final rush toward us. Peter, the dog, and I huddled, knowing we could do little more than wait for the end.

He nearly reached the boat when a great sucking in of the sea preceded the powerful breaching of the great white whale. Full he breached from the sea, and full he fell on Godwin. The fiery eyes of the Narwhal went blank as his back broke . . . he was dead.

Beyond relief, we sat in the boat, numbed by the proximity of death and the violence of action. Only then did I notice that Harmony lay oddly still in the water, the dead Narwhal very close. Around them, the water grew slick with blood. The great, evil, twisted horn had run Harmony through, lancing out his back. But the weight of the now-dead Godwin caused the ivory horn to slowly but sickeningly pull free. The Narwhal dropped down like a spiraling leaf to the end . . . the beginning.

Without thought, I leaped into the water and swam to Harmony. "Why," I signed, "why risk all for a sandwalker?"

"Because," he softly sang, "the Narwhal is right. If the sandwalker can learn to sing the Song of the Sea and to grasp its full meaning, there is hope for whale and sandwalker alike. There is a tradition with the whale that the song must be carried by a scribe, a recorder, of the Song of the Sea. The scribe must never be involved but instead must stand off and watch and record so that nothing will be lost from the song. I was a scribe, a recorder, but I stepped away from my responsibility and became very involved for a time. I now pass the song on to you, Sharing, so that you may sing it to others."

With reverence, he began to sing the most wondrous song I have ever heard, the history of the world through the heart and soul of a whale. I listened to the song of Harmony. From Harmony, I heard the song of Laughter Ring and finally heard my own song . . . Sharing.

When he finished, he softly cried, "Go, Sharing. Go to the dryside and sing the song to any who will listen. Do not cry for me. Many, many tides ago, I loved and lost my love to the dryside. I now go to where she waits."

He slowly began to settle in the water. Floating down to the crystal-cold waters below, his last words were, "Oh Melody, how I loved you. I now am part and parcel of the song." And with that, Harmony joined the end . . . the beginning.

I drifted on the surface of the bay. Peter and the dog watched, not fully understanding but surely feeling empathy and compassion for the moment. I finally swam back to the boat and, with Peter's help, crawled over the water-slick sides. The oars long-since lost, we paddled by hand the long journey back to the dryside. We had to circumvent the glacier, since traversing it would have required more effort than we had strength. Our dear friends, Laughter Ring and Little Brother, again came to our rescue. Always playful, they nosed the small craft along the icy shore and pushed it scraping up on the gravelly beach.

They were joined there by the bustling bundle of energy, Giggles, and as they began to swim away, Laughter Ring called to me, "There is a place called Winsome Bright, and there lives a wonderful Beluga called Momma Love. If you seek us or need our counsel, she will know where we are. In unison, they swam into the shimmering midnight sun.

Hours later, Peter and I were rescued by a group of very curious environmentalists and a gaggle of reporters and taken back to the little town of Gilroy. We have been here now some three months, and I have transcribed all of the song as best remembered. As a sidebar, a tiny melody to an already complex symphony, Peter and I were married the week after the conclave. Bonded as we were already by the events, it was only natural that we bond for life. He has heard the song, and I have heard the song; once heard, it must be sung. We now sing the song for any who will listen.

Now it is late, and tomorrow we will begin a journey that will last our lifetime. I came out to walk the beach alone, to gaze at the now-empty sea and to wonder at the grandeur of it all. The night is not bright, but well lit nonetheless, in this early northern fall. Cotton-gauze clouds filter the half-moon light as I walk my silent walk. Mercury waves slip and slide like long, twisty snakes, hissing up and down the pebbled shore. The air, cool and crisp, bites at my cheeks and explodes into silver vapor

streamers as I exhale my breath long-held. This is Alaska September, fall in a place of early hard winter. I look back to where the gravelly shore refuses to mark my passing with lingering bootprints. It is as if I were placed where I am coming from—nowhere—having nowhere to go.

I am now of the Song of the Sea, for I have heard it sung. I am the one in billions of humankind who must try to teach the others to sing. Should I fail to do so, mankind will earn the punishment it has so freely passed on to others . . . extinction. Like my bootprints, we will leave no trace on the jagged edge of the dryside near the waters of life.

If you hear the song, sing it again and again. Fear not the Narwhal or others who, for their own narcissistic devices, do not choose to listen, let alone sing.

May you find Harmony in the singing of the Song of the Sea.